ONE FELL SWOOP!

John S. White

Inspired by true events

This is a fictionalized account of a true event. Any resemblance to actual persons, living or dead, is purely coincidental.

Publisher:
AAPS Publishing – Oklahoma City, OK
ISBN: 978-0-692-86320-6
Card Catalogue Number: 2017904760
Title: One Fell Swoop/ John S. White
Formats:
Digital distribution | AAPS Publishing, LLC, 2017.
Paperback | AAPS Publishing, LLC, 2017

DEDICATION

Two places my heart will never leave, Oklahoma and my beautiful wife Kim. This is for both of you.

PROLOGUE

Before two elephants disappeared for nearly a month during the summer of 1975 in Oklahoma, you may ask yourself, what were two baby elephants doing in *Oklahoma!* to begin with?

To answer that, we have to go back to 1942, when a local business man with a fascination for the "Big Top" saw value in having a famous traveling tent circus reside in Hugo, a small town of 6,000 residents in southeast Oklahoma. He lured one from its home in nearby Mena, Arkansas with an offer of free rent and utilities in exchange for showing their animals on Sundays.

During the years that followed, more than a dozen traveling circuses made Hugo their winter headquarters at one time or another, earning the town its billing as *Circus City U.S.A.*

Hearing the lions and tigers roar in the distance or having clowns, tight rope walkers and trapeze artists speak during career day at Hugo High School has kept things interesting. Even the cemetery has a special plot known as Showmen's Rest, with colorful and creative headstones placed in an area where only circus people are buried.

Each year, Hugo's leading industry leaves town for several months to entertain families everywhere across North America. While they're gone, local church collections shrink, businesses sell less clothing, food or auto parts and feed stores feel their absence most of all.

While one of the circuses was on a short mid-summer break in Hugo on July 10, 1975, two baby elephants barely two years old, Lily and Isa, decided to become not one, but *two babes in the woods*. For more than three eventful weeks, they outsmarted and outlasted hundreds of searchers among the dense hardwood trees, heavy thickets, lakes and streams of Southeast Oklahoma, in what became known as *The Great Oklahoma Safari.*

CHAPTER ONE

1:34 pm, July 10, 1975

Roland Hill believed the horizontal state, where he was at the present moment, should be represented on the American flag with the 51st star.

That platform would most likely get him elected to some kind of office in Little Dixie, a moniker that refers to his remote region of Southeast Oklahoma. Around here, many of the residents considered that being just down-on-their-luck was pretty good considering most had no luck at all.

At the moment he was nowhere close to an office, not that he would know what one was, but as usual, he was making one of his regular afternoon visits to his favorite state. His current delicate condition was a byproduct of his desire to manufacture the area's best tasting moonshine which, as always, required an ample amount of *tastings.* To his long complaining wife Margaret, he spun the black outs as a professional hazard.

Amid his repose, there was a sudden loud CRASH, several gigantic THUMPS, followed by an even louder second and third CRASH and, finally, the sound of a large volume of liquid SPLASHING on concrete. The crashing alone sounded like train cars derailing on the Frisco Railroad tracks that ran along the barbed wire fence just a furlong from Roland's small white framed farmhouse.

The melee outside had little effect on Roland, causing him to simply roll over, the shift causing the vinyl on his sofa to mimic the sounds of passing gas. These were sounds that Margaret could never really distinguish from the real thing while she was in the kitchen baking apples and broaching the cherries that would eventually be added to Roland's Mason jars. Upon completion, Roland's "shine," as he referred to it, resembled unlit Molotov cocktails and usually had a similar incendiary effect on one's brain.

He fluffed the worn feather pillow as his head came to rest on his left side, then made a smacking sound twice before drifting back asleep.

CRASH, THUMP, SMASH...it repeated again and again and again until Roland's bloodshot eyes popped wide open. The sunshine that filled every corner of the room necessitated squinting at the front door. Placing his hand over his eyebrows as if to salute, he peered at the television set across the room and saw it was off. Now partly awake, he felt the urge to pee, sitting up ever so slowly and rolling his feet to the floor. With both hands, he pushed himself up and off the sofa, the vinyl farts harmonizing with the real ones he streamed as he stood up.

The journey to the bathroom was thankfully short and took Roland by the living room's open window which offered a view of his gun metal gray barn and verdant rows of corn dominating his 160 acres. He stopped for a moment, absorbing the light cooling breeze wafting in and brushed away the dirty linen curtain which had come to rest on his shoulder. As his eyes came free from his dirty hands he'd been rubbing over his face, he saw it. It? Them? Huh? Roland's first words he uttered could just as easily equated with how he felt, "What the hell? Margaret!"

No answer. She had gone into Hugo, the nearest town with a grocery store.

Roland took a couple of steps back from the window, his foot suddenly astride an empty Mason jar on the floor, sending him toward a hard landing against the wall. He managed to break his fall by catching himself on the arm of the weathered fabric recliner nearby. He crept back to the window and peeked out toward the barn, which was really more of a large shed, and this time he saw it. It? Them? Or, was it nothing? Again he screamed "Margaret!" forgetting she didn't answer the first time.

"Roland, Roland, Roland," he muttered to himself and snorted out what sounded like a wet snicker. "That latest batch is some of your best shit ever son."

He rubbed his hands through his thinning brown hair and looked around for the empty jar. It had safely rolled to a corner, assuring a clear path to the bathroom. Except for one small bump into the side of the door jam, he managed to stay vertical long enough to void himself, before returning to America's newest state in the union.

It was the strong aroma of alcohol in the crest of the breeze coming through the window that woke Roland up again. This time for good.

CHAPTER TWO

One hour and 47 minutes earlier...

Sherriff Burke Blakemore was surprisingly elected to office with very little prior experience as a lawman in Oklahoma. Having been raised in Hugo, what Burke did possess was a considerable knowledge of Choctaw County's topography and geography which came in handy when stalking the *cookers and growers* of a couple of the area's largest revenue producers, moonshine and marijuana.

A sturdy built man in his late 40s with a bit of a paunch, thinning hair covered with a white straw cowboy hat and bearing the olive complexion of his Indian ancestry, Burke could have easily been mistaken for any other rancher in the county except for the shiny gold badge on his white cotton shirt.

On the morning of July 10, 1975, he could have fried an egg over easy on the hood of his truck, the time and temperature on the Citizen's Bank clock at the corner of Jackson and Broadway showing 11:21am and 101 degrees. At the moment, he was making his weekly drive to Holton's Sale Barn, where cattlemen congregated each Friday to buy and sell cattle on the east end of town.

Following up on a call regarding a domestic disturbance, he made a quick detour before getting to the sale barn, going north of the John Deere implements lot. His mission was to determine if John Hunter's truck was parked at least 1,000 yards away from the front of his ex-wife's house, as the court had ordered. Molly Hunter's restraining order on her former husband, a stocky red haired ex-Marine with a flat top and fiery temper, was a constant source of repeat calls to the Sheriff's office and was the cause of repeated visits to their small farm home. When he arrived, Hunter's yellow 69 International Harvester pickup was nowhere to be seen.

He swerved into the gravel driveway, grinded his 1974 Ford Bronco with 3.5 Monster Suspension into reverse and rolled the left tires through the slight culvert back onto the road tossing dust and gravel over the Hunter's fence as he sped off. He slowed briefly a half mile away as a White Tail Doe chased her fawn across the road about 60 feet in front of him, each jumping the fence and disappearing immediately into the heavy thickets of brush on the other side.

It was another ordinary day for the new sheriff in an otherwise ordinary town and his mind turned quickly to the Sale Barn hamburger he would soon be having for lunch.

CHAPTER THREE

The presence of Rose and Hahn as well as several other circuses which wintered there, allowed the town of Hugo to stake its claim as "Circus City USA!" and gave the Chamber of Commerce another arrow in its quiver.

With it being ten days into July, all of the circuses had already left their sprawling grounds outside the city limits, with caravans traveling to the far reaches of North America to entertain and enthrall hundreds of thousands of kids and their families.

Rose and Hahn were on a short break after performances in Minnesota, Iowa, Missouri and Kansas, with stops in Texas and Mexico up next. Pausing for a few days in their home town, situated conveniently in-between, gave them a chance to rest the animals and visit loved ones. As a special treat for the local community, they had erected the "Big Top" in order to perform in front of town folks before continuing their journey south.

Like many circuses, and especially the traveling kind, they romanced the towns once they arrived by walking the elephants and wild animals in horse drawn cages down the main street before raising the mighty three ring tent to a height of sixty feet or more. Typically, the kids came to watch this pre-show and some were lucky enough to earn free tickets by running errands and doing odd jobs for the crew.

Lily and Isa were elephants headquartered in Hugo as part of the Rose and Hahn family. They lived there along with other elephants as well as lions and tigers and bears, leading a fictional character in another story by the name of Dorothy to exclaim "Oh my!" when faced with a similar set of circumstances.

They were barely more than two years old, still infants in an elephant's life span which was generally 60-65 years in captivity. Both were a little over five feet tall and weighed 2,000 pounds each, only about half the height and a third of the weight of their adult counterparts.

Once the circus began, the two trained elephants along with others, performed amazing tricks such as standing on their heads, balancing on one or two legs, dancing, rolling balls into nets and even riding bicycles. But no one who had ever watched circus elephants perform had seen them disappear. Until today.

CHAPTER FOUR

On this sweltering summer's day, Lily, Isa and Juliet, a 30 year old adult elephant, were on the circus's grounds, being prodded into picking up the tent's heavy steel poles by handlers using bull hooks, small sharp pointed steel rods. Rolling the poles into their trunks and using their might, they placed them onto the back of a long flatbed truck, an action that had become almost second nature to them.

Several in the circus crew were nearby, folding pieces of the mammoth canvas tent which had been flattened out on the ground to dry. A couple of others were on the truck's trailer stacking the poles.

Playful as ever but feeling the heat, the three elephants were allowed to stop frequently for water and shoot each other by streaming it through their trunks. It was work as usual for the well cared for females, which were usually chosen oven male elephants for circus training because of their preferred behavior patterns.

Juliet, although much older, stronger and more experienced than Lily and Isa, still shared something in common with them; they were learning to react to a new trainer. The one that had raised them, a kindhearted circus lifer known as "Jungle Joe," passed away the previous winter and was ceremoniously buried alongside fellow circus people in a dedicated area known as "Showmen's Rest," in Hugo's Mount Olivet Cemetery.

Without Joe's familiar and soothing voice, the elephants, especially Lily and Isa, had shone a recent tendency to become wary of humans and frighten more easily. Wade Hammonds, a former assistant that had been recently promoted to head trainer, was taking it slowly with them, knowing they would need a little more time to adjust.

Wade had just given the elephants a break from pole stacking and was standing on the other side of the 18 wheel flatbed trailer, smoking an extra long Marlboro Light with Shirley Ray, a 50-ish year old stocky woman with curly red hair in skin tight Wrangler blue jeans, long sleeve plaid shirt with the sleeves rolled up and Wellington boots. Known as "Curly," she was a veteran truck driver for the circus's sole owner, Buster Rose.

After the break, one of the workers on the trailer reached to grab his end of a steel tent pole, letting it suddenly slip from his grasp and causing a large stack of them to roll off the trailer. They loudly clanked against each other as they bounced at the feet of the elephants.

The frightened elephants, agile despite their enormous size, bolted as if circus daredevil performer Günter had shot them from his cannon. Wade and Curly reacted immediately, running to the other side of the truck, but were powerless to do anything but yell at the elephants to stop. Wade tried whistling for them to halt, although he didn't know why as they hadn't been trained to respond to a whistle. Perhaps at this moment, not even an oncoming missile could have stopped them.

Frightened elephants can run at a speed of 25 miles per hour, travel great distances at 10 miles per hour and easily walk 3-6 miles per hour. They were already at cruising speed and no one in the gallery watching them flee had the ability to catch them on foot. Even if they did, they couldn't stop them unless the elephants managed to calm down and stop on their own.

Miraculously, that's just what Juliet did. Older and apparently wiser than Lily and Isa, Juliet must have instinctively known that the direct heat, dry creeks and rotted roots that lay ahead wouldn't compare to the berries, sweet hay, coconuts and corn she enjoyed in her climate-controlled stall.

If that was actually what she was thinking, Lily and Isa lacked those spontaneous analytical skills while crashing through the four feet high cyclone fence next to the road. Still startled, they were running somewhat slower because of the bruises encountered from the fence. However, their gait showed no intention of stopping anytime soon.

What the stalled out Juliet would not know was the fact that Asiatic elephants in the wild can consume up to four times as much food in a day than those in captivity. For Lily and Isa, their swift freedom would momentarily have its advantages, it was time to ditch work, have some fun and pig out!

CHAPTER FIVE

Isa had an impetuous nature and seemed to take charge immediately. Instinctively, she thrust her trunk as high as she could into the air and began adjusting it side to side and behind her to sense the presence of enemies.

She paused momentarily on the scorching asphalt street, the pressure sensitive nerve endings in her feet detecting the vibrations of distant automobiles. Spooked by this, she eyed a clearing on the other side and again picked up her gait. One thing was certain, she had no frame of reference for what she was sensing in front of her or even for what she felt in her feet. Had she looked behind her, which was an impossibility for an elephant unless she made a complete stop and turned a 180, she may have instantly recognized the non-threatening presence of Wade still running toward the smashed fence or the trailers parked in rows, one of which was fully padded, air conditioned and protection for her thick skin from the summer heat. However, when one is impetuous in nature, whether a pachyderm or a human, it's all the same. She acted quickly, without thought or care, moving forcefully ahead.

Barely 600 yards into their escape, Lily was rumbling, grunting and squealing slightly. Not used to running any kind of distance, there was little doubt she needed to take a blow and had expected her grunting and squealing to communicate that desire to the new leader of this wild herd of elephants in Oklahoma.

Wasting little time, Wade, who had ran a hundred yards in hopes he could convince them to stop, ran back to the truck, jamming his thumb slightly as he tried to swiftly unhook the tractor from the flatbed trailer. Jumping into the passenger's side of the cab, he motioned for Curly to climb in behind the wheel, a process she was already in the middle of doing. She turned the key, slammed the stick shift on the floor into gear and spun the rear tires while headed toward the front gate.

"What in the by-God has gotten into them two Wade?"

"They're just scared. They won't make it more'n a quarter mile before they're down rollin' around in a mud bog."

"Don't cha think we ought to call Mr. Rose?"

"No need for that, we'll get 'em shortly," Wade said somewhat distractedly.

Curly turned left outside the gate, driving the section line road going east of the circus grounds, tracing the southern boundary of a square mile of a forest loaded with thickets, cedars and post oaks tangled in vines.

"Slow down some," Wade instructed as he bent forward, putting his hand to the bill of his cap to shield his eyes from the sun.

"They gotta be hearing us and it's spookin' 'em even more," Curly said. "Want me to shut the engine off and we walk?" It was at that moment Wade saw what he thought to be the ample tush of one of them.

"There! Over there! They're headed north through them bode arc trees!" Wade exclaimed. Bois d'arc trees sported formidable thorns capable of ripping through clothes and into the hide of humans as well as the sensitive skin of elephants.

"That ought to get their attention," Wade said, "after a few of them thorns they'll be beggin' us to take'm home."

He was wrong. Undeterred, the smaller size of the two baby girls slid easily between the trees and their massive hooves stretched and snapped the thickly curled vines that attempted to attach themselves.

"ON-GAH-WAH!" Wade screamed while swinging the truck's door open and leaping onto the road before it had even rolled to a stop.

He launched himself to the edge of the fence and with his right hand cupped to the side of his mouth shouted "ON-GAH-WAH! ON-GAH-WAH!"

"On-gah-wa?" Curly asked to Wade's back, "*Tarzan?*"

"ON-GAH-WAH!" Wade shouted again not answering. "ON-GAH-WAH!"

"Yeah, I got it from watchin' *Tarzan* movies as a kid. Hang on. ON-GAH-WAH!"

"I've been tryin' to use it to train them two since they're still young. I figgered it'd be kinda entertaining, maybe make an act out of it."

"Is it supposed to make'm stop?" asked Curly, showing what looked like a hint of amusement. "Maybe it'd help if you was wearing one'a them buckskin tutus."

"Yeah, well, it ain't stoppin' 'em, so maybe I need one."

"Tarzan could always make his echo," Curly replied. "Maybe you should learn to do that."

"It's supposed to call'em but I hadn't worked'em long enough where they know it yet," Wade said ignoring her last statement.

Using his lean six foot four, one hundred seventy pound frame to step cleanly over the barbed wire fence, he navigated a path into the woods by bending under the low hanging branches and stepping over the myriad of rough leaved dogwood bushes.

Moving in the direction he thought they were headed, he stopped for a moment to listen for any sounds of feet rustling through the leaves or branches snapping. There was complete and utter silence.

Curly placed her elbow on the unopened door of the truck and leaned out the window, "Where's the real *Tarzan* when we need him?"

"There ain't no real damn *Tar Zan* Curly," Wade said disgustedly.

Although she heard him, she couldn't see him.

Within a few minutes, Wade reluctantly tromped back to the truck, coming around the front of the hood, stepping up and in. He was convinced they would find Lily and Isa before dark based upon the fact it was still early in the day. However, he knew they were going to need a lot more help.

"Now we call Mr. Rose?" Curly asked.

"Nah," Wade said curtly. "First, let's drive to the next road and take a left, maybe we can cut them off before they come free of this section." he said, his eyes still trained on the area where he had caught the last glimpse of them. "They ain't eat nothing, they'll git hungry pretty quick, probly stop soon as they catch'a whiff of some Muscatines or blackberries."

Curly restarted the engine and sped up the road quickly. Both of them were distracted and didn't see an oncoming blue Ford pickup, causing Curly to jerk them back to their side of the road as she heard the long blare of its horn. The pickup went left into a shallow culvert but managed to steer back onto the road and on its way, but not before the driver held his left middle finger out the window.

Curly noticed it in her rear view mirror and Wade saw it in his side mirror but both could care less. They didn't take time to consider how lucky they just were because at the moment they weren't having any luck at all.

"What are we gonna do when we do catch up to'em?" Curly asked. ""We ain't got no trailer. We just gonna get on their backs and ride'm back?"

Wade gave a half smile at the thought but by now was looking north after they turned the corner.

"At least you have a sense of humor about this," Wade said. "We git close enough for them to hear my voice, they'll stay with me."

They were now a little more than a mile from the circus grounds.

"You want out and I'll go get the big van?" Curly asked, referring to the enclosed semi-trailer that Lily and Isa shared.

"Too soon for that. I'd like to see'em first. Get their attention."

"Shhhhiiiiitt!" Wade suddenly uttered, making it a three syllable word and drawing it out until it was an exclamation. Ahead 20 yards to his right, he spotted a tangled barbed wire fence and four wooden posts lying over.

"They're out dammit!"

Lily and Isa had crossed a second section line, headed east into the next square mile of unimproved farm land, another 640 acres of exactly the same wild mass of vegetation they had just dealt with.

"Now we call Mr. Rose," Wade said.

During the drive back to the grounds, Wade recalled another incident with one of the elephants two years before.

This wasn't the first time an elephant had wandered off from the circus grounds. The last wayward mammal wound up in Iris Coker's back yard only a few blocks away, rubbing the bark off one of her native pecan trees, then sucking the ornate birdbath dry while basking in the shade.

Iris, upon seeing the elephant through her kitchen window, first grabbed her broom to shoo it off only to think better of it and call the Sherriff's office. A neighbor with five acres next to her, seeing the elephant standing around, grabbed a square bale of hay from his shed and dropped it over the fence into Iris's yard. That was all it took. She happily pulled clumps of hay off, curling them up into her mouth until the circus staff arrived.

Wade knew this time was going to be considerably different. There were two instead of one and he could add to the fact they were jarred loose of their senses. There was no telling when they would relax. In the case of their predecessor, she was mostly curious about some children playing in the street south of the grounds and moseyed out an open side gate while nobody was paying attention.

With Lily and Isa having already crossed their second and maybe by now their third section line, the search area had widened to four and maybe even nine square miles. Wade's optimism for a swift return of the elephants by the end of the day was waning.

CHAPTER SIX

As Curly and Wade pulled onto the grounds, Manny Elizondo was sitting in the tractor that was attached to the elephant's van. They pulled alongside.

"I been waiting to hear something boss," Hector said in mostly clear English, having been raised in Oklahoma. He had attempted to locate Curly on his CB radio.

Curly, known on the highway to users of CB as Red Rubber Ball, realized she had not had her radio on. The oversight, even if it was in the heat of the moment, had her miffed.

"You gott'em corralled boss?" Manny asked Wade, appearing relaxed with his left arm on the window frame.

"All we have right now is the direction they're headed."

"I need you to take your rig down Kirk Road and turn left at the corner. Then wait there," Wade said looking out the driver's side window past Curly.

"Is that where I pick'em up?"

"Not yet," Wade answered quickly. "Once they got back in those woods we lost 'em. Just wait there."

"Got it boss," Manny said, putting the truck in gear and heading toward the gate.

Curly continued to the barn, loading several bales of hay in the back of a five year old Dodge Dude D100 pickup truck.

Wade climbed into a green and white Ford F100, hoping the 10 year old truck would start. It had seen better days but at the moment it was the only choice he had.

He told Curly and another worker named Frankie he was headed back to where they had seen the downed fence. Curly and Frankie were to take a separate path, going north of that spot and then east. He was hoping the elephants had slowed to rest, still close enough to the road that they could surround the section in question. He took one of his assistant handlers and dropped him off on the road to the south and handed him a mobile radio. He looked down at the CB under the dash to make sure his was on.

They would now have all four directions in view. If they emerged now someone would be there to spot them. He was confident the elephants would settle in once they found a food source and water.

The rest of the plan would be pretty simple, rely on the combination of an elephant's keen olfactory nerves along with their storied memories to bring them closer once they got a whiff of the sweet hay and watermelons that Curly and Frankie were lining the road with. It would be as close to the smell of home cooking as they could get.

Once they came to the road to gorge themselves, Manny would have their trailer ready and gently command them back into it using his bull hook, a process that had been repeated with them dozens and dozens of times.

As Manny idled north along Kirk Road, he spotted a path through a cornfield where the six foot high corn stalks had been laid flat. Once he stopped for a closer look, he could see that the path turned into two separate paths before crisscrossing and becoming two again, forming a figure eight.

"Trunk Boss?" Manny called out on his CB, "This is Merry Mex. Over."

"Yeah, go ahead Merry Mex," came Wade's response.

"What's your 10?" asked Manny, meaning Wade's current location.

"Kirk Road."

"Copy that. I'm a half mile north of Kirk," Manny reported. "They headed through a quarter section of corn and it don't look like they stopped to pop any."

"Shhhiiitt! Shit! Shit!" Wade shouted, coming loud and clear through the CB speakers of Curly, Frankie and Manny plus anyone else on their same channel.

"You think they're headed east? Over."

"They are," came the reply but from Curly and not Manny. "The fence is busted over up here near the northeast corner and there ain't no fence across the road. They haveta gone in there."

The radio was silent for a moment as the realization that this was going to take reinforcements, as many as a dozen or more, was beginning to land hard on Wade. He thought about what he was going to say to Mr. Rose.

A search into deep woods at night would be nearly impossible. Although it wasn't uncommon for people to hunt in these parts at night, especially those illegally jack lighting for deer, it would not be smart to do so. The two elephants could easily run further away if they were frightened by night sounds.

With the search expected to span as many as 16 square miles of mostly dense vegetation, they would have to enlist enough people to pull an all-nighter along the roads, hoping they would miraculously appear out of nowhere.

Wade drove first to look at the cornfield Manny had described, and then found Curly. Along with Frankie, she already removed the hay bales and melons from the previous section line and was baiting the new stretch of road.

The latter part of the afternoon was beginning to cool a bit, the sun going behind a gathering of high Cirrus clouds.

After another hour of patrolling and baiting the roads, Wade left the others and headed to Rose's house.

CHAPTER SEVEN

Rarely is a jail break spur of the moment. Inmates have plenty of time on their hands to plot the perfect escape and even more importantly, they notify accomplices to determine a safe passage before they are on the outside.

Lily and Isa had no such plan.

What they had, at least for the moment, was a forest bed full of *horse apples,* the round, five inch wide, yellowish green fruit of the Bois d'arc tree. Actually not related to apples at all, they are more remotely related to the mulberry.

Lily and Isa rolled them around and snorted the bumpy exterior of these strange objects until Isa curled one up into the tip of her trunk, stuffing it into her month. As the milky white latex-like juice exploded from the fruit, it oozed out each side of her mouth, sticking to her four molars like gauze. Lily instinctively reached the tip of her trunk over to Isa's mouth for a quick smell, picked a tiny piece from the corner of her upper lip, then returned with it to her own mouth.

Anybody watching these two starving mammals curling horse apple after horse apple into their mouths would have sat somewhat amazed. As plentiful as horse apples were in the Red River basin, the taste and texture of the fruit, although edible, were not preferred by humans or animals alike.

As Lily continued to gorge, Isa flapped her ears suddenly forward. Elephants possess the ability to smell humans from as much as a mile away and can hear other animals for up to two miles. The sound she heard in the distance was one of rustling at first and then a much more worrisome series of loud and angry snorts.

Isa was familiar with the pet sounds of the many animals kept in cages by the circus. She had also become used to the familiar humming of water coolers, the squeegees atop the mop buckets used to swipe her van clean and the clasp of sliding doors which offered her mindless protection from the outside world. However, this sound was unlike any of those. The knotted and twisted stand of 40 to 50 foot tall Bois d'arc trees, while providing a formidable barrier around them, offered no sense of security at all.

Isa backed toward Lily, her head facing the direction of the noises and soon the two were turning together and heading in the opposite direction. If they had any second thoughts about their earlier swift run to freedom it would be now.

They alternately walked and lightly jogged for a couple of minutes, their fears lightening up with each step. The direction they were headed had them on a north and east track, putting additional distance between them and the Rose and Hahn grounds.

CHAPTER EIGHT

The previous experience had made them a little more wary of their surroundings. Continuing to travel cautiously and quietly, they were careful to avoid limbs that would crack and reveal their location. Their arched backs slid under the low lying limbs easily brushing them back and they remembered to veer away from the long thorns that grew on the spine of the Bois d'arc leaf. They were figuring things out quickly, simply because they had to. Had they been Cub Scouts, they would have qualified for a Tiger Patch, the first rank for completing basic adventures.

Their trek was taking them through a shady grove of trees before spilling out into a small clearing, the bright sun blinded Lily momentarily and the sound of that angry snorting thought to have been left behind had once again appeared, stopping her dead in her tracks. She raised her trunk and widened her ears, an instinctive move that was supposed to evoke fear in her rival. Isa was to her right, her left ear slapping simultaneously into Lily's right ear. Once they were able to focus they found themselves surrounded by a sounder of feral hogs, known as Razorbacks. Their leader and the fiercest of their pack was the lone wild boar, which was rooting with the 30 or so sows through the downed corn stocks around them.

Razorbacks mimic the activity of sharks swimming in the ocean. They rarely stop, and usually sleep for only two hours before they're back rooting and destroying. They tear up wheat fields, obliterate pecan groves, feast on baby deer, turkeys and even calves. Some may grow as tall as four feet and they always possess a nasty demeanor.

Lily and Isa didn't possess a frame of reference for the kind of animals they had just encountered. They only knew they were right in the middle of them at this moment.

Several of the females began to lodge loud threatening grunts toward the two intruders not really concerned with the fact that either one of the elephants could make 10 of them. Lily and Isa stood completely still, seemingly content to just watch and listen until several of the other females left their husks and began to close in, leaving their piglets behind them.

Until now, Lily and Isa could only smell the raw odor of their potential enemies, their small eyes offering them only a minimal distance for seeing clearly. As the hogs moved their 200 pound frames closer and closer, Lily and Isa began switching their weight from side to side, raising their trunks as a sure sign they were ready for battle.

Had a few of the sows only flashed their razor edged canines and tried to bluff them with their grunting, perhaps Lily and Isa would have ignored them and gone on their way. It was the wild boar charging out from behind the pack of sows that changed that potential outcome.

With his head down and sharp, four inch tusks ready to thrust upward into his foe, the 400 pound hog charged as straight and purposeful as a torpedo toward Lily's right front leg. Although boars have killed prey as large as deer, a confrontation between a wild boar and an elephant was surely the world's first. Now extremely agitated and frightened, Lily took a step back swinging her head and trunk back and forth like a pendulum, erecting a steel curtain between her and the rampaging beast. As he dove for her leg, Lily's trunk caught him flush, like a bat meeting ball, sending the squealing pig airborne. He plopped to the ground, rolling fifteen feet until he could right himself.

Not one of the other hogs came to his defense. Instead, they stood as if dumbfounded. The massive boar rose to his feet, shook his head to clear it and repeated the direct charge technique that had never failed him before now. He didn't have time to find out if attack number two would work. Isa bolted from her stance behind Lily's right flank, charging directly at the startled pig in a game of chicken. The hog dug his hooves into the ground and for the briefest of moments felt himself completely shaded from the sun before seeing the massive leg of Isa bend 90 degrees at the knee, crushing into the top of his skull.

The sounder had already seen enough, most of them retreating into the trees the first time their leader went flying. What few that were left scattered quickly.

Isa stood over the flattened boar, sniffing his carcass to determine if there was any challenge left in him. Lily began flapping her ears and made a slight gesture toward the sows, sending them running further into the trees.

The two were nearly exhausted, the panic and subsequent struggle had mixed with the heat to take a toll on them. They each raised their trunks into the air almost simultaneously as if to celebrate triumph, but in reality they were hoping to replace the smell of victory with the smell of water.

Going back to their stalls for food and water after a performance under the Big Top had never offered a moment's peril for Lily and Isa. In less than a day, they had already realized that moving from one meal to the next in the woods would be rife with challenges.

Chapter Nine

Their instincts had them locked into heading in the same direction as before their altercation. They crossed the remaining rows of depleted corn, heading again into the trees for shade and resuming their search for water. A nice farm pond would do. There were plenty of small and large creeks that striped the county but by the middle of summer, most were bone dry.

With each passing step they were becoming more acclimated to their environment as they moved further and further away from their servitude in the circus.

After a quarter of a mile, they came upon another corn field approximately the same size as the one they had escaped into previously. Ignoring their growing thirst, they grazed upon the standing husks of field corn, unknowingly doing severe damage to the livelihood of the farm's owner.

Their walk through the rows of corn had actually done far more harm that what they could eat. Emerging from the six foot high stalks, they saw a gray shed, about the size of half a house trailer and not unlike the many they had seen situated around the Rose grounds.

Sensing they may have found their way back *home,* they kept their gaze focused straight ahead while strolling to a fence where only one wire strand stood between them and the shed, a small white wooden farmhouse and the weed strewn yard.

Lily touched the tip of her trunk to the wire first. Immediately rearing up, her front feet came a few inches off the ground as the 5,000 volts of electrical current zapped into the boneless mass of flesh. The surprised elephant, as if stepping back up to a bully's challenge, no longer sought the use of her trunk. Her small ivory tusks, sans nerve endings and better yet, not a conductor of electricity, snapped the wire in half.

They stepped forward cautiously into clumps of clover and cottony five inch high dandelions, whose seeds began to spread into the breeze created by their passing.

Their noses had them making a beeline for the smell of water coming from the shed setting 90 feet from the house. As they approached, the tiny hairs on their backs began to stand when they heard what sounded like dripping water. Walking around the perimeter of the well fortified shed, the metal structure had two thick, dead bolted doors. It only took two swings, one from Lily and one from Isa, to knock the bolts loose from the jam.

Pushing the door open with the crown of her head, Isa stepped inside. It was plenty large enough for each elephant and sufficiently cool, but unfortunately no water in sight! However, they could still hear it dripping, seemingly coming from below them.

The soles of their feet detected a slight vibration beneath the bare ground where they stood and as Lily stepped forward, there was a locked metal door laying flat. With one solid stomp, the door gave way, the two stepping to each side of the hole to avoid falling in. After the loud crash, they were looking down their tusks at several large copper pots with tubes running out of one and into another. That sweet aroma of water was conjoined in this particular case with *sugar, cornmeal, yeast and malt.*

Thirstily, the girls reached their trunks down into the hole to smell for a source, then flicked the lids off the pots. They began filling their trunks with what tasted like honey dew vine water. Consuming upwards of a gallon a draw, the elephants enjoyed their new found shelter from the heat and the *hydration* they had been looking for.

CHAPTER TEN

Finding two girls drunk and alone in a bar would have normally been a Godsend for Roland Hill. However, these weren't normal girls and the sight of two elephants standing in his ransacked still house was more than he could process at the moment. The fact they had all but completely drained the main source of his livelihood hit him even harder than the hangover.

Once he snapped too, he realized there really wasn't anyone he could call. Certainly not the Sheriff, as a moonshine still the size of his was a one-way ticket to the gray bar hotel, especially considering he already had a prior conviction. What the hell elephants were doing here and how they got there came to mind. Surely their owners or somebody was looking for them. Could they be nearby?

He walked away from the shed toward the dirt road, looking up and down it for a sign of anyone coming. Nothing, not even a dust cloud.

The only thing he could think to do was grab a few pots and pans from the kitchen and bang them together hoping to startle the two interlopers. It worked for shooing skunks off the porch so why not elephants?

"Okay guys, last call!" Roland bellowed as he pounded the frying pan into the sauce pan. "Get the hell out of here and don't forget to tip your waitress you sons a bitches!" BANG, BANG, CLANG, BANG...

Reacting to the sudden banging, the frightened elephants lost track of the situation, resorting to their senses that detect danger. They turned for the door, hastily liberating themselves from the sound of metal clanging for the second time in one day. As they exited their *private lounge,* they took out the remainder of the décor as well, including several stools, a work bench and numerous shelves.

They hustled in the direction from where they had originally come, through the same gap in the electric fence.

Roland reluctantly chased after them a few feet before stopping to watch the hilarious sight of two drunken elephants, rumbling, stumbling and tumbling through his corn stalks, staggering back and forth in front of one another before finally disappearing.

According to Margaret, Roland's sense of humor was about the only sense that God had given him. He would need it now as he stood there wondering how he was going to explain this to his State Farm agent, coming to the conclusion he wouldn't and couldn't. On this one, he'd have to absorb the cost of the damages himself.

Now completely sober, Roland recalled the vision of the two elephants he had thought were a figment of his imagination. "Ho-lee shit," he said to himself.

It was precisely at that moment that he became depressed. Not as much from the destroyed distillery but from the knowledge that his most recent batch of *'shine* wasn't nearly as hallucinating as he had thought.

CHAPTER ELEVEN

There had never been anyone with the circus with the name Hahn. It was actually a name Buster Rose had made up because two names sounded better then one. He was currently in the air conditioned office of his stately ranch style brick home on the northeast edge of Hugo, plotting the upcoming trip through Texas and Mexico.

Wade had driven through the Rose's front gate so many times he seldom paid attention to it. Today, the irony of two silhouetted images of elephants on the bars reminded him of the dread he felt at having to face Mr. Rose with the news. As confident as he was in the prospect of finding them quickly, he was troubled by the fact that their animals would be in danger if they remained loose overnight.

Before heading to Rose's, he had placed as many of the circus hands available along the pertinent roads and even some volunteers from their families. Some were handed what available two way mobile radios were on hand. He would borrow others if necessary from the Highway Patrol or Sheriff's office. He monitored the chatter between his lookouts hoping he would have a positive sighting and location to assuage the distressing news he was about to deliver.

He followed Rose's circular drive around to the back the house, shut off the engine and rapped once on the back door where his office was located. After a few seconds, he pushed it open without waiting for a response.

Buster Rose, a distinguished looking six foot tall medium framed man with thinning gray hair, was standing at his conference table, in the process of confirming the routes the circus would take on the Texas and Mexico portion of their tour. J.W. Milton, the circus's general manager, who some thought looked like Rose's twin brother, was seated near him.

"Hey Wade, come on in here and cool off," Rose said, looking at him over the top of his reading glasses. "Big day tomorrow, we about to get those tents struck?"

"There's a bit of a problem," Wade said, ignoring Rose's question.

Rose slipped off his readers and looked at Milton who was looking at Wade.

"Problem?" asked Milton.

"Two of the elephants, the young ones, Lily and Isa, we're tryin to find'em now."

"Trying to find them?" Rose asked calmly.

"We've been lookin' for the past several hours, they got off in the woods and..."

"They've been out for several hours!" Milton half shouted. "Why didn't you call us?"

"I didn't think we needed to. We thought we'd get'em back pretty quick."

"Apparently you haven't," said Rose. "Do you have an idea where they are?"

"Curly and I followed'em as long as we could, then they started crossin' section lines, and got outta sight."

"Well you can't lose two damn elephants for several hours when they simply walk off the..."

"...They didn't walk off," Wade interrupted. "They ran off."

"They ran? From what?" Rose asked.

"They were loadin' tent poles on the flatbed, Lily, Isa and Juliet, the ties snapped and they rolled off right in front of'em."

"It only took a second and the three of'em were gone in one fell swoop."

"Three of them, you said two," Milton interjected.

"They went straight through the fence, Juliet stopped after they got on the road but the other two never even turned around."

"Well I'll... be... damned," Rose uttered, in the process of sitting down.

"I never seen anything like it Mr. Rose. They took that fence clean out. I have about 20 people out there searchin' the roads."

"Just the roads?" asked Milton.

"The problem is the woods. None of those sections are farmed, just timber, brush and thickets."

"So the idea is to wait them out?" Milton said. "Who has time for that? We leave tomorrow morning."

"It's okay J.W., we want to make sure they're safe," Rose said. "We can do without them for a little while if we need too."

"Let's just go find them before they do get themselves hurt," Milton replied, looking at Wade.

"Which way did you say they went?" Rose asked as he began walking toward the door.

"East of the grounds, angling to the north."

"And they've been gone how long?" asked Milton, his furrowed brow and frown showing the concern he had.

"Five hours."

"If it's been five hours they're gonna be hot and tired." Rose said glancing at Milton while he said it.

"They're out there looking for water, you can bet on that," Milton said.

"And no one has seen them for five hours? Not one person that lives around there?" Rose asked, his voice rising with surprise. "You'd think someone would spot two damn elephants in their pasture!"

"Other than corn rows, they hadn't been headed toward open pasture," Wade answered. "They stumbled on the perfect stretch of woods to get lost in."

"Have we got enough people out there looking for them?" Rose asked.

"Yes sir, as many as I could find," Wade said. "Hopefully they're standin in someone's front yard waitin for us to come git'em right now. They've never been alone much less outside their cages for more than a few minutes without someone around."

"Maybe so...but if that's so then someone would have called you on that radio hanging on your belt," Rose countered.

"I have at least 20 of our people out along the roads." Wade reminded them, relieved that he had the search party arranged before it became Rose's idea. "We've baited the roads with hay and melons. Manny's parked nearby with the big van."

Milton walked over, putting his hand on Wade's radio, slipped it out and put it to his ear. "Manny? Manny? Over!"

"Try Merry Mex," Wade suggested.

Miller rolled his eyes, "Merry Mex? Over."

"Merry Mex. Over," came the immediate reply from Manny.

"Manny, how we lookin? Anybody see anything?"

"Not yet Mr. Milton, not yet, but you know we will."

"Where are you now?"

"I'm on 93 about three miles north of the highway." Manny reported, meaning he was three miles north of U.S. Highway 70, which cuts east to west though the center of the county.

"That's the last direction they were headed, north and east. They've left a few entry points into the woods but few trails," Wade offered.

"There are quite a few people that live in that area," Rose said.

Milton, almost forgetting they had been talking with Manny, put the radio near his mouth, "Okay Manny, we'll get back to you. Over."

"There's a thousand ponds out there and they could be soaking in one of them right now," Rose said not knowing if he was exaggerating or not. "We could use a map of the county."

"If they stay on that northwest course they'll run up on Hugo Lake," Milton added.

"They won't make it that far," Rose said.

"The lake would be a good thing," Wade said.

"You're right. They'd only have two directions they could go at that point," said Milton.

"The county extension agent or the Sheriff's office will have a topography map," Wade said, changing the subject quickly back to Rose's earlier question.

"The county agent's office closes at five, it's past that now," Milton said.

"He's got a home phone," Rose said sternly, the frustration beginning to show in his voice.

CHAPTER TWELVE

Lily and Isa were soon back beneath the thick stands of trees, the cumulative effect of their canopy providing a respite from the sun but not the heat. Humid Choctaw County was the epitome of 92 in the shade during the middle of summer.

Their heads and eyes were not yet clear from the gallons of moonshine they had consumed. The constant movements that healthy elephants are known for were decreasing rapidly, to the point of listlessness. Even drunk, they managed to notice the thicket of blackberry bushes only a stone's throw away, the smell of the berries helping them to refocus. What could be more perfect for two girls with the munchies!

Without regard for the fact that this year's blackberry preserves and cobblers would be severely limited for some farm family, they completely stripped the bushes by tying their trunks around each limb and ripping them off. There weren't enough to fill them up but it didn't matter, they were tired to the point of sleepy and the snack was enough to put them out.

Elephants will take short naps standing up but contrary to popular belief they don't sleep standing up. Lily was the first to lie down. First she squatted on her front legs then her back and rolled to her side with a thud. She was out before her head hit the ground.

Isa walked over to Lily, touched her tenderly on the neck with the tip of her trunk as if to check her pulse then joined her with a thud of her own.

Lily had fallen asleep so deeply her legs were kicking involuntarily. Isa was snoring!

It was unusual for them to sleep during the heat of the day. Back *home,* in their vans, the normal pattern was to take brief naps, awake from them and then sleep again a few hours before dawn. However, a typical day back home never consisted of several miles of jogging, gorging on all-you-can-eat produce, a fight to the death and Happy Hour at Roland's.

So much for Wade's prospect of finding them in a farm pond before the day was over.

CHAPTER THIRTEEN

After 30 years of living in Choctaw County, Rose knew it was not the kind of place to be combing through the woods at night. It was an easy way to get your head blown off by an overly cautious landowner or suspicious operator of one the county's scores of suspicious still operators or pot growers.

As a precaution, he ordered the crew to continue their watch from the roads while staying put. In his estimation, it was only a matter of time before his two fugitives would end up within someone's field of vision.

He called Sheriff Blakemore's office to alert them of the situation and to the possibility of a phone call from a resident pinpointing the two elephant's where-a-bouts. He assured the dispatcher that the Sheriff's services were not necessary.

It was nearing dusk and most of the volunteers had long since abandoned their posts in search of supper. The long afternoon and evening were taking its toll on the circus crew left and Rose gave each of them, sixteen in all, the option to go home and come back at day break or sleep in their cars and trucks. Half of the group remained, taking turns keeping vigil through the night.

The hours between sundown and sunrise were uneventful; nothing what-so-ever had stirred the landscape. The radios and the phone lines remained silent except for the occasional chatter between the posts.

Rose and Milton showed up shortly before dawn with coffee and donuts, delivering them from vehicle to vehicle and handing them to the others as they began to arrive. He inquired about the elephants as he visited each, asking them to keep their voices to a whisper and any other noise to a minimum. He had to tell one crew member to turn down his car radio.

Knowing the sleeping habits of elephants as well as he did, Rose was surprised with the lack of nocturnal sightings. While most elephant herds will certainly move in the night, he theorized these two most likely wouldn't since they were used to nights in their vans with the whirring sound of tires on asphalt to help them doze off.

With the new day about to dawn, he was certain they would be up and energetically seeking breakfast near someone's farm house.

By holding the crew's positions, Rose felt it would at least afford them a more advantageous starting point for the second day of the search. In his mind there would not be a third day necessary, nor could they afford the time as the circus had to roll out on Sunday.

Milton had mapped two adjacent areas, each comprised of four square miles, as the most likely places the elephants could or would have stopped to rest. He arranged the crew members into pairs, spread them out and had them begin the arduous task of climbing over fences, squeezing through thick groves of scrub oak and evergreen trees, and tromping through waste-high thickets covered in vegetation. Before they left, Rose reminded each to be on the lookout for ubiquitous bushes of poison ivy with the same admonition his mother would tell him as a boy, "Leaves of three, let it be."

It was 6:00 A.M. and already hot as a branding iron.

CHAPTER FOURTEEN

Lily and Isa awoke at first light. The two dehydrated pachyderms worked slowly to their feet by rolling over until their front legs were positioned at the top of their abdomens. Then, in what was more like a heave than a push, they were up.

Where were the buckets of cool water usually thrust over them by Johnny, their trusted caretaker? The tubs of clean, fresh drinking water and bales of hay always at their disposal? What, no breakfast in bed today? These strongly ingrained visions of home were quickly banished once shafts of sun burst through the openings in the tree tops. Almost in unison, they placed their trunks into the air, turning their tips right and then left. The scent was almost immediate and it was close!

Within three hundred yards of their bed was breakfast, a field of watermelons, green and yellow striped Black Diamonds and Charleston Grays, which were more olive drab than gray. With only a barbed wire fence stapled to wooden posts standing in-between them and the all you could eat buffet, they each leaned their two front legs against the wire. The barbs caused superficial cuts but nothing so serious that they had to abort the mission.

At the west edge of what was five acres of Leon Johnson's sweet ripening melons, they began rolling up their trunks before dropping them onto the tops of the melons. THUMP! SPLAT! Just like that, melon after melon was bursting open, splattering into large chunks. They rolled the sweet meats of the melons, rind and all, into their dry mouths, the sweet juice squirting out like water from a sprinkler. For a half hour they grazed their way across the patch.

Oblivious to their surroundings, at least for the time being, Isa quit in the middle of a chew, flopping here ears forward as she heard a strange squeaking sound. She glanced toward Lily as if it may have come from her but saw she too was exercising her cautious nature, her trunk stiffened horizontal to the ground and straight ahead. It was straight ahead indeed. Ninety feet away was a leaking water pump handle attached to a metal pipe protruding from the ground. The water trickled down the metal pole portion of the pipe and near it were several identical pumps lined up about 30 feet from each other.

Leaving the carnage of rinds behind, they began walking toward the leaky one, Isa putting her beady left eye as close to the orange handle of the pump as possible. The orange represented nothing to her, looking as black and white and gray to the color blind mammal as the rest of the pipe. What did register was what happened to lie beneath this protruding *tree? Weed? Or was it a vine?* It made little difference, *it* was water!

With one blink-and-you-would-have-missed-it left to right swipe of her trunk, the pipe was sent cart-wheeling across the patch leaving a flume of water gushing several feet into the air. The joyous elephants stood momentarily posing in the self made rain before darting in and out of the cooling spray with an agility that they had yet to demonstrate until now. Isa straddled it to cool her under belly then stepped aside for Lily to do it as well.

The two began taking turns putting their mouths over the spray until they had to back off to breathe. Before long, Isa spotted the other pumps close by and soon had her own shower.

CHAPTER FIFTEEN

Leon Johnson loved early mornings. A short, sturdy and friendly black man in his mid-fifties, he frequently came out and sat on his small concrete patio covered with a corrugated tin overhang. Usually he'd sit quietly, watching the sun clear the trees to the east before casting a bright golden haze on his watermelon patch.

There was no telling how many ripe watermelons Leon had setting in the field at this moment, but he knew today would be the most he would haul into town this season. With his wife Louise, who was a bit on the pleasantly plump side but fit from loading and unloading 10-15 pound melons, they would take their 15 year old Chevrolet pickup into the field, load the bed full, and drive them to local grocery stores, farmers markets, roadside stands or wherever anyone was ready to buy. They would do it several times all day long, every day until all were gone.

On weekends, they would load the back of his pickup and sell them for two dollars apiece alongside Highway 70, the pink juicy meat catching the eye of campers and boaters on their way from North Texas to the beautiful mountains of Beavers Bend State Park in McCurtain County. Getting retail price as opposed to wholesale, it was usually a very nice cash payday for the hardworking Leon. A former Gunnery sergeant in the Korean Conflict, Leon loved his country, but he never shared any of the proceeds with Uncle Sam.

With a piping hot cup of coffee in hand, he pushed open the screen door with his elbow, feeling the burst of morning heat on his face and arms. *Wait! There!* Straight ahead Sergeant at 12 o'clock! Water was gushing 30 feet into the air right in the middle of his patch, accompanied by the completely baffling sight of two elephants bounding around in the sprinklers, their enormous size and gray color reminding him of enemy tanks in the distance. At the moment, he could actually conjure up kinder thoughts about the North Koreans than the two invaders stomping on his livelihood at two dollars a pop!

He began shouting as he ran several steps toward the beasts, stopping several hundred yards away. "Hey! Hey! Wudda ya'll think your doin'?! Go own! Git outta there!" He screamed it as if it were common to see elephants in his patch and scaring them away with loud screaming always did the trick. He reared his right arm back, slinging his cup toward them, sending a rooster tail of coffee across the ground directly in front of him. The cup rolled to a stop only 300 yards short of the intruders.

He turned, running toward and through his screen door. He returned before it even had time to close with the .22-220 varmint rifle he kept loaded by the back door to shoo away deer and other watermelon thieving culprits. He raised it to his right eye, sighted in the scope and within seconds had Lily in the cross hairs. He placed his finger on the trigger and "Leon! Wudda ya doin' out there with that gun?" Louise boomed through the screen door.

"Gonna shoot me some elephants," Leon said with a calmness that belied what he was feeling inside.

"Say what?"

"You looks out there, yule see'm."

She stepped outside on the patio, still rubbing the top of a white dinner plate with a red dish towel, "Whut you gonna shoot them for?"

"Dey tearin' up my field," he replied with the rifle still leveled on Lily.

"Don't do that Leon," she said firmly. "You know they gotta be from one of them circuses in town."

Leon stood still a couple of moments longer before coming to his senses, raising the rifle up and shooting off three rounds into the air. BAM! BAM! BAM!

Just as Roland's pots and pans had done the trick, the sound of Leon's rapid rounds firing had them heading for the nearest exit, taking out another 10 foot section of Leon's fence.

Escaping with their hides intact, the elephants disappeared into the trees, cruising beyond Leon's sight in seconds.

Had Rose or anyone of his crew heard the shots, they would have most likely surmised it was a local farmer responding to the fear associated with seeing the elephants close to his property.

However, the report of a .22-220 can't be heard from as far as *three* miles away.

CHAPTER SIXTEEN

Leon carried his rifle over his left shoulder like a harpoon as he walked across the patch, past the smaller melons still ripening on the vines and toward the devastation the elephants had left behind. He really hadn't taken time to consider the likelihood of a manhunt in progress or that a phone call could save others from the same fate as him. In fact, he spent an hour walking around, checking the busted water lines, leveled fences and eyeing the hundreds of melons that had been devoured or stepped on.

He retrieved the banged up pipes with their handles still intact and tried unsuccessfully to replace them on the shafts that were left. Now soaking wet, he stood and walked 250 yards to the main water valve, twisting the round wheel on top counter clockwise until it shut the pumps off.

Afterward, he walked slowly back to the house, his anger rising as quickly as the heat. He reached down and picked up the coffee cup laying among the vines, walked a few more steps, then jerked open the screen door so hard it snapped the bottom hinge off the jam, leaving it hanging almost parallel to the ground.

Cheryl, the dispatcher at the Sheriff's office, was a heavy set young woman with a pile of ratted brown hair placed atop her head. The phone rang three times before she picked it up and found a not so calm Leon Johnson asking to speak to the "cheriff."

"I'm sorry, Sheriff Blakemore isn't on duty today Mr. Johnson. Is there something I can do for you?"

"Who's on dooty?" Leon asked as firmly as if he were talking to a lazy Private in his platoon.

"Just a second, let me see if I can get Deputy Mullin."

Deputy Wayne Mullin was not in charge, no one was but the Sheriff. However, he was in the office and answered the phone.

"This is Deputy Mullin."

"Depidee, I got a big problum out here!"

"Out where? Who am I speaking too?"

"Leon Johnson. Out here at my melon patch!" Before Mullin could ask what the problem was, Leon continued. "Dey wuz two eliphunts terrin' up my whole patch jus a little bit ago."

"Elephants?" the deputy said. He held his hand over the phone and quickly asked Cheryl, "Do you know anything about any elephants that got away from one of the circuses?"

"No." Cheryl replied with a quizzical look on her face.

"Okay, Mr. Johnson. If you saw elephants on your place, you need to hang up and call someone at the Rose Hahn circus. I know they're in Hugo at the present time."

"Whut do ya mean if I seen elephunts? No if 'bout it. I knows whut I seen and dey dun tore up my patch an my fence. I wanna press chargiz! Dey costing me a bunch a muney."

"So you want me to arrest two elephants?" Mullin said wryly, "What do I do then, hoof print'em?" He was looking over at Cheryl who had her mouth covered laughing.

"You think I's jokin' wid you? Cuz you shore jokin' wid me!" Leon was now getting even more infuriated. "I need dem folks dat own'em to pay me for what dey dun!"

Mullin assured Johnson he'd either come by or send someone to investigate and write a report. As soon as he hung up he asked Cheryl to get Rose's phone number. He dialed it twice but didn't get an answer.

Cheryl kept looking at Mullin as he sat on the edge of the wooden desk with his hand resting on top of the phone. "Burke said he was going fishin' this morning." she volunteered. What she really meant was, if he's thinking about notifying him he's probably not home.

Mullin, in his forties, six foot even with a medium build and wearing a white straw Stetson, stood and headed outside to his police cruiser, a black and white 74 Dodge Monaco. He planned to run by Rose's office on the way to Johnson's farm. *Elephants loose where Leon Johnson lived?* The concept made very little sense to him, knowing Johnson lived several miles east from the circus grounds.

CHAPTER SEVENTEEN

It was obvious the circus grounds were cleared out as Deputy Mullin drove up. Just in case, he shoved the cruiser into neutral, left the motor running and knocked on Rose's front door. After waiting a few seconds with no answer, he pulled back on to Kirk Road and headed toward the turn that went north on 93.

State Highway 93 was a straight two lane of which Mullin knew every stretch. It eventually curved along the northwest corner of Hugo Lake, an area that reminded him more of Louisiana Bayou country than it did Oklahoma. He had spent several Friday and Saturday nights chasing off local high school kids that were lined along the narrow shoulders of the highway watching friends illegally conduct drag races. The sight of his flashing red light was usually enough to disperse them quickly. Sometimes, just for fun, he would gun his 440 cubic inch engine, roaring up behind the two side-by-side racers before flashing them to pull over. He would never report any of the kids to their parents but always warned them if he caught them again they were going to jail.

The Rose Hahn semi-trailer was parked a couple of hundred yards down a gravel section road about four miles north of 70 on 93. Mullin turned onto the road, driving alongside the tractor which was empty at that moment.

Manny came around from the passenger side still zipping up his fly.

Mullin spoke first, "I hear ya'll are missin' a couple of elephants?"

"Yes. Yes. You seen them?"

"I just heard about it. I'm on my way over to Leon Johnson's place. He apparently has."

"We bin out all night...I wait 'til they call. That's good. Somebody call." Manny's accent was always more pronounced when he was tired.

"You know if anyone is out near Leon Johnson's place?"

"I do not know who that is?" Where he live?"

"Not close to where you are," Mullin said, giving a wave and rolling up the window, "You better call someone and get over there. I better get going. If you need directions, call me on channel 13."

Manny notified Wade, who in turn notified Rose. The two of them, along with Milton, were already at Johnson's house as Mullin drove up. There was a sense of relief expressed by Rose, to have had their first *official* sighting since the brief glimpse Wade had just after they had broken free.

The circus crew had already congregated in Johnson's drive causing Mullin to weave in and out past them as he drove toward the house. Mullin's gaze fell upon one person in the crew as he sat on the side of a pickup's truck bed in a full clown uniform complete with a wild orange wig but without face paint.

He stopped and stepped out of the cruiser, glanced back at the unpainted clown then asked, "What's with the clown suit?"

"These are my girls," the clown replied. "This is the only way they know me."

Without saying another word, he put his straw hat on and walked over to where Johnson was having a heated exchange with Rose, Milton and Wade. He had already heard it once on the phone, so he walked around them and waited.

Rose acknowledged the deputy by cocking his head backwards as he peered at him. "Hello Wayne."

"Lose something?" Mullin joked.

"We're getting closer to finding them," Rose replied, refusing any small talk. "These are our two youngest ones and we apparently underestimated the ground they could cover. Mr. Johnson here had a visit from them this morning."

"So I heard."

"We think they could be going due east toward the lake," Milton said.

Wade tapped Rose on the shoulder, apparently nervous and ready to go. Johnson could only point in a direction he saw them run. Otherwise, he just wanted assurances he would be paid.

The men concluded their conversation promising to send someone out to fix Johnson's fence and hydration fixtures as well as bring him a fist full of free circus tickets for his melons. Johnson could be heard protesting that settlement attempt as they walked toward their vehicles.

Once inside the car with Milton, Rose muttered "Well hell, I guess it's no longer just a circus matter."

"We'll find 'em today. With the word getting out, it won't be long before we'll have them pinned down," Milton said, sounding as if he had snipers positioned in the hills around them.

Certainly, none of Lily and Isa's pursuers had any idea of the kinds of things they had already experienced. Little did they know the two pampered elephants were no longer afraid of their own shadows and already adjusting to life in the wild.

To everyone except Rose, they were two lost souls looking for a way back home.

Rose's experience with elephants made him think otherwise. The longer they were loose, the more they would want to remain that way. They could quickly adapt to their surroundings and apparently were already doing so. It made perfect sense for them to gravitate toward the lake, no doubt they could already smell it in the distance.

He wasn't quite ready to admit it but he knew a more military style effort was needed, complete with a base of operations.

CHAPTER EIGHTEEN

At 4:00pm, the temperature had peaked at 98 with 70% humidity. That index coupled with the demanding terrain and expanding circumference of the search area was beginning to take a quick toll on manpower. The wider each group fanned out and the further down the roads they went offered no visible signs of Lily and Isa.

Rose had begun characterizing the elephant's actions as *hiding* in conversations he was conducting with people that lived in the area. At least he hoped they were only hiding and not purposely running further away.

After the Johnson episode, the subsequent excitement of their closing in had been quelled by the fact they hadn't been seen since. The several hours that had passed seemed more like days. Some of the crew searching the woods east of Johnson's patch reported several places where bark had been rubbed clean on trees but little else.

The question kept popping up, how could these two behemoths get away so cleanly?

It was decision time for Rose and Milton. The circus had contractual obligations for several Texas venues and Mexico City, and the caravan of tents, performers and animals had to be on the road the next day. That would require pulling all but a few of the crew from the hunt and getting them on their way. It also meant asking for more people in the community, the county and the Sheriff's office to get involved.

Fortunately, the contract didn't specify how many elephants were required to perform in the show and it was looking as if the opening street parade of showmen and animals on their way to the Big Top would be minus Lily and Isa. The Rose and Hahn "prayer ring," where six elephants would kneel in a circle, would be reduced to four. The clown act that required Lily and Isa to surprise them with huge sprays of water before being playfully chased around the ring would be cancelled.

Milton and Wade began contacting the affected crew members to beat a retreat back to the grounds where they would be waiting to put the finishing touches on the trip.

With the heat, confusion and general frustration continuing to exhaust everyone, none in the crew were disappointed when relieved of their duties, except Willie, the clown with the crazy orange wig whose solo act was cancelled.

Although Wade would be on hand to ready the entire troop for departure, he would remain in Hugo for a couple of extra days with Curly and one of the assistant animal trainers, Chuck Wheeler. They assured Rose they should have the elephants located by the next day.

If indeed the next day were the case, with another day to allow the elephants to re-acclimate into their familiar surroundings, they would be on the road only 24-48 hours behind the others.

After supper, Sherriff Blakemore and Deputy Mullin arrived at the Rose home along with Walter White, President of the Hugo Chamber of Commerce; Rod Perry, the County Commissioner for district two which comprised where the elephants were currently residing; local newspaper publisher Jeff Post and J.D. Little, a former professional rodeo steer wrestler and currently the operator of the annual Hugo PRCA Rodeo.

Rose was in his conference room, already seated at the table with Milton, Wade and Wheeler as the rest of the group filed in within minutes of each other.

"I guess you were frying up all those fish you caught for supper?" Rose said to the Sheriff as he sat down. "Where'd you go?" Rose himself was an avid fisherman.

"We were telephoning them from a flat bottom boat on the Red River," Burke joked, waiting for Rose's reaction to a law enforcement officer illegally electrocuting fish.

"Then you must be fishing with Garrett!" Rose said, a reference to the county's most notorious illegal fisherman. Selling fish that were telephoned or caught in nets was against state law but Mike Garrett made a decent living doing it.

"We've been setting and running trotlines at the lake," Burke replied, referring to the legal practice of stringing heavy nylon fishing line clear across coves and baiting the attached hooks with live shad, minnows or gold fish. "We'll go back and run'em again around midnight."

Rose followed his conversation with Burke with a round of small talk with White and Perry, and then gave a brief explanation of the situation. In summary, the elephants were still hiding somewhere in the woods; the circus troop had to bug out leaving them short of searchers and he concluded the overview by sharing his latest concern. He was worried his valuable elephants would eventually go north, circumnavigating the natural barrier the Kiamichi River and Hugo Lake presented. If they took that route it would take them into Pushmataha County, an even larger and more remote wilderness with small mountain ranges, an area he described as an *elephant Shangri-la.*

As a point of clarification, Jeff Post mentioned Hugo Lake and its 110 mile circumference of shoreline as the most likely target for the two, a fact that was already obvious to everyone at the table.

"There won't be a Monday gentlemen," Rose said firmly. "We need to wrap this up tomorrow."

Burke agreed and added, "It would be a better use of what manpower and equipment we have if we begin the search early Sunday morning on the west side of the lake, then work our way back toward the elephants."

"You're basing that on the assumption they will be headed east." Perry said. "What if they headed north like Buster said they might?"

"We can put a couple of people along 93 up there."

"I don't know if we have a whole lot of choices," Rose said, responding to Burke's strategy of starting west and heading east.

White rolled out the Chamber's large topographical map of Choctaw County and Hugo Lake. Burke immediately took charge, pointing out the roads where vehicles should be positioned and recommended a spot for an air conditioned RV with a kitchen to be placed in order to serve as the base of the operation. The volunteers staffing the RV would function as headquarters gathering any and all pertinent information to plot on the map. White promptly volunteered to remain in the RV, weathering a few barbs from the others about his eagerness to avoid sweating his ass off with the rest of them.

"It's my RV," White said. "And I'll have Mary out there cooking."

"That's a deal!" Little added quickly. White's wife, Mary, was well known with the rodeo hands around Hugo for her delicious country style cooking.

Little was a vital asset, not only bringing his life long experience of living in the county but as President of the Hugo Riding Club, he promised to recruit as many of their members as possible to organize *posses*. Once it was determined where everyone would meet on Sunday morning, he left to begin making phone calls. Sunday was most people's day off and he felt confident he could engage as many as they needed.

"Gents, we gonna have ourselves a real live posse!" Mullin said after Little exited the room. "Except the two outlaws we're lookin for ain't exactly Frank and Jesse James!"

Mullin's silly comment had newspaper man Post scratching out notes on the pad he had in front of him. "I have an idea," he said, flipping his pad closed and making a hasty exit through the door.

"What's your idea?!" Mullin half shouted as Post was leaving. He never replied.

Ignoring Mullin, Burke, an excellent horseman as so many were from these parts, located a point on the map near the southern end of the lake and determined he should lead a three mile wide in-line sweep utilizing some of the volunteers from the riding club.

"I hope they wear their chaps," Burke opined, "Riding through that brush country on horseback will rip the jeans clear off their legs."

Burke's reference to the difficulties to be faced for the riders was prophetic for the elephants as well. Lily and Isa had already found out the hard way. The stinging from the cuts and scrapes had become commonplace. Untreated, these kinds of wounds on elephants could become dangerous very quickly. Even an occasional prick or scratch could become infected and lead to a life threatening abscess.

Such occurrences were usually tended to immediately by their handlers, using clean water first and then applying Iodine and a healing salve of Chamomile Extract. Without the services and skilled nursing they received at the circus, they instinctively began washing each scrape whenever they came to water and gathered mud with their trunks to apply to the sores.

Before Rose's conference ended, it was determined that Wheeler and Curly would bring two large vans, each capable of hauling one of the elephants, to park along the route. Then, they would move them north or west as necessary to keep pace with the horsemen.

Rose was no fool, announcing his plan to join White in the air conditioned RV. He would also plan to make periodic drives into the surrounding area himself, alerting residents in the area to be on the lookout for not only the elephants but the men on horses that will be cutting across their farms and ranches.

Milton and Wade had little to add, instead sitting preoccupied in thought over the *things to do lists* that would need to be completed for the circus's launch that next morning.

It was dusk when Burke walked out of Rose's house, on his way back to his office in the two story red brick and concrete court house located near downtown. His route took him by the newspaper office as Jeff Post was walking out the front toward his car. When he motioned, Burke pulled over.

"Workin' late Sheriff?" Post asked, knowing the answer.

"Looks like you are too."

Post put his hand on top of the rolled down window. "Don't you find this whole thing a bit hysterical?" he asked with a large smirk on his face.

"Oh it's kinda funny but it'll be a lot easier to laugh about it once we find'em," Burke replied. "I'm hoping we get lucky tomorrow. No matter what, it's gonna be a lot of work."

"Makes a good story Sheriff."

"I guess it probly will sell a few more papers for ya Jeff, I didn't really think about it that way."

"Well, compared to the garden club story and the photo of the ribbon cutting for the new payday loan office that was on the front page today, I think more people will be willing to drop a dime on the counter to read about a couple of tame elephants slipping off to the lake for a little *skinny dipping*."

"Skinny dippin?" Burke questioned. "More like *chunky dunkin.*"

Post laughed loudly, tapped Burke on the forearm and began to walk away. "I may use that one!" he said. "See you bright and early, Sheriff!"

CHAPTER NINETEEN

Rose slept restlessly, waking up several times throughout the night. All he could think of was that they had to put an end to this today. There was each animal's safety and health to consider; another concern was the volunteers would only have one day off so time was of the essence. The dent it put in the show was weighing on him but most of all, his babies were valued at over $20,000 a piece!

Arriving at the Horse Club's designated meeting site two miles east of the lake, Rose felt a charge when he saw a large group of riders assembling. It was just before dawn and most had white Styrofoam cups of steaming coffee in their hands while they stood near their horses or trailers talking.

The 5-10 mile an hour breeze made the present 82 degrees feel more tolerable. One of the horsemen exchanged pleasantries with Rose as he walked by and mentioned "we're ready to go, Mr. Rose!" He knew he meant into the woods, but it wouldn't be long before he would mean back to his paying job on Monday once he realized this was not going to be fun.

Imagining what was ahead of them for the day, he considered the possibility for injuries as he made his way toward the RV. Once inside he made a note to have a paramedic and ambulance on call.

He had made coffee and was pouring a cup when White stepped in. "Buster, are we ready?" White asked just opening a conversation. He loved to talk.

Rose liked White but found him to be a bit flamboyant, this coming from a guy who ran a circus! Flamboyance in this case was a critical quality, it made White the quintessential salesman. If he wasn't already an insurance agent and President of the chamber, he could easily be a candidate for a barker in one of Miller's midway games or better yet, the Master of Ceremonies in the center ring.

Burke, dressed in leather chaps, a thick long sleeve cotton shirt and yellowish tan Resistol hat, walked around inspecting the horsemen. He was relieved to find most were dressed the same as him, including leather boots with snake covers and riding gloves. The gloves would offer protection from the head-high, sharp-edged Johnson grass that was capable of slicing into a finger when trying to whisk it away. The chaps would fend off the thorn bushes and poison oak along the way. With all of the clothes necessary, the heat was going to be another factor.

The more experienced riders in the club had two metal canteens strapped to their saddles, sheathed 40 ought 6 rifles for snakes and beef jerky in their saddle bags. They clearly lived for stuff like this. As Burke paired people together, he attempted to put one of the lesser experienced *Cub Scouts*, as he referred to them, with the *Eagle Scouts,* meaning the veterans.

Satisfied with the group as a whole, he grabbed a cup of coffee from the metal coffee pot on the campfire and headed toward headquarters to quickly go over strategy.

"Hey Burke, you know why those two elephants probably won't be out there in that lake swimming?" asked White as soon as the Sheriff's head appeared in the door of the RV.

Not really understanding the need for the question, he tersely replied, "No."

"They only have one pair of trunks between'm!" White bellowed then began snorting he was laughing so hard.

"Good one Walter, did you get that off a Bazooka gum wrapper?" Burke said, looking amused while glancing at Rose, who even chuckled a little at White's joke himself.

Mullin poked his head in and said Little had called for "Riders up." There were 22 in all, not counting himself, Burke or Little. He informed them that Chuck Wheeler had located an alternate driver for his truck and was also planning to join them on horseback. "Any change to the marching orders?" he asked looking at Burke.

Burke looked at Rose as he stepped past Mullin on his way to the riders. He was already shaking his head side to side. "No," Rose said.

He began by expressing his appreciation for each of them taking time away from their families, church and any other usual Sunday activities to be there. Rose chimed in from behind him as well, "Free tickets to the circus for you and your families next year!"

"And cotton candy?" One of the riders asked jokingly, making everybody laugh.

Burke told the riders they would be spread out about a quarter mile apart or about four pairs per mile. He sternly warned them to make no attempt to capture the elephants if they spotted or cornered one, or both. There was no need to tell them that a physical encounter with a 2000 pound animal would end badly for anyone attempting it.

"All of us will have our walkie-talkies set on the same frequency." Burke instructed. "If you don't have one, we have extra ones."

"If you see tracks, trails or signs of foraging then report it so all the groups can be aware and we'll keep a record of where it is here on the map."

"Hopefully, once we see enough signs, we'll begin to have some kind of pattern or a trail to follow."

"How we gonna know if those trails are the elephants Sheriff, and not some big ole hog or buck?" asked one of the riders.

"Just look down, your horse will probably be standing in a hoof print the size of a tire," Burke answered, causing a wave of small chuckles through the group. "If you have reason to think the track looks fresh, then by all means follow it and we'll steer the others in your direction."

"Does anybody have any questions?" Burke asked as he was putting his foot in the stirrup and crossing his leg over the back of his horse.

"A lot of us ain't never tracked nothing bigger'n a coon or a coyote Burke," a rider named Butch remarked, making more of an innocent statement and not really asking a question.

"There ain't much to trackin' elephants Butch," Mullin chimed in. "Just climb off your horse, hide in the bushes and make a noise like a peanut." The comment put a grin on Butch's face and drew several more laughs.

As Burke started to make a hand motion to send the riders packing, he caught a glimpse of a short shiny steel rod with a hook strapped to the side of Wheeler's saddle. "What's that Chuck?" he inquired.

"Bull hook," answered Chuck. "When we find them we may havta control'em."

"That thing's nasty looking,"

"Well, I doubt anyone is going to be able to rope'em."

"Looks like you're gonna piss'em off even more. We may never catch'em if you go flashin' that thing around."

"Call it a situational hazard Sheriff," Rose volunteered matter-of-factly as he stood on the steps of the trailer.

The riders tapped their spurs against their horse's flanks, leaving to the sound of steel horse shoes crunching the gravel. As they sauntered by, most took a peek at Wheeler's steel pointed bull hook glistening in the angry oven heat of the July sunrise.

The terrain on which they were riding proved to be near-ly impassible at times. There were several false bottoms underneath the tall grass that left several of the riders bruised and battered from repeated spills.

The riders were navigating around as much as they could, spreading even further apart. Paying attention for signs was problematic and there was yet to be one sin-gle clue that indicated the elephants had passed through their areas.

After four hours, the inexperienced Butch was one of a dozen riders that eventually began to turn around and work their way back to the RV. The heat was too much and they felt very fortunate that none of their horses had been injured.

Stopping for a quick break under a stand of blackjack trees, Burke and the remaining 12 riders left on the trail were reassessing their strategy via their walkie-talkies.

He was yet to consider the effort to be a failure and, given time, they should be hearing something from peo-ple living or farming in the 40 square mile area they were attempting to cover.

With Highway 70 and it's passing cars and trucks forming a barrier to the south, that left the unbounded area to the north, where the lack of structure would of-fer no interference if the elephants were inclined to head for the mountains as Rose had feared. Burke figured they would begin from the north tomorrow and head south along the river and lake if they didn't find them today. Of course, he didn't personally share that thought with Rose.

Burke sent Mullin and another member of the posse to follow the road south of them, one that dead ended in Hugo Lake State Park. Mullin joked that it would make matters a lot simpler if a park ranger would just happen up on the two escaped *youngsters* in the park's play-ground sitting on the teeter totter.

The remainder of the group had to work their way around an almost mile long arm of the lake in order to reach Salt Creek Road, meaning they had now ridden almost five miles and more than likely had zigzagged twice that. They had paid particular attention to the shore line of the lake but saw or heard nothing.

If the elephants had indeed made it anywhere near the point they were currently standing, the engine roar from the Sunday boaters or the squeals of children would have surely run them away. Perhaps a quiet fisherman anchored in one of the coves would get a glimpse of them.

Burke radioed the RV, requesting they come give them a ride back to where the horse trailers were parked. It would be quicker and easier to bring the trailers to the horses. Everyone, especially the horses, needed a break. A third day of disappointment was coming to an end.

Waiting in the RV for the rest of the posse return, Rose and White exchanged ideas for what to do with the remaining daylight. Rose suggested they spend the remainder of the day visiting as many people in the area as they could. Another suggestion was to contact leaders of the local scout troops, hoping they could have their kids pass out flyers to area residents, churches, schools, country stores and to cars passing on the roads. White accepted the responsibility and expense for printing the flyers and contacting the scout leaders.

Burke made it back with the others and received commitments from nine of the riders to meet him the next morning at the wide cove near the north end of the lake, known as Messer Point.

Burke's phone rang as he walked in his house, a reporter from the *Dallas Morning News* wanting to know if what he had heard was true regarding two elephants gone missing for three days.

"I have no idea what you're talking about," he said, then hung up and fell backwards across his bed.

As if Hugo didn't already have enough circuses, one more was about to come to town; *the media circus*.

CHAPTER TWENTY

REWARD OFFERED FOR RUNAWAY ELEPHANTS!

The *Hugo Daily News* trumpeted the headline in a Monday morning edition. Normally published in the afternoons six days a week, Post thought the story was too good to wait, summoning his editorial and composition staffs in on Sunday evening to make the new deadline.

Regardless of the fact that Post had not bothered to clear it with anyone at the Sheriff's office or with the circus, the newspaper was offering $150 to anyone providing information about the elephants which would lead to their capture.

It was day four and for the first time, people all over the county realized the rumors were true. Two of Rose and Hahn's prized elephants were actually on the loose in the county!

The morning coffee cliques at Best Café downtown and Tyler's located on the city's east side, were foregoing their usually subdued table conversations about someone's infidelity or lamenting about cattle prices, to read lines from the story to those that didn't have a paper.

Over the top of the buzz, in a voice loud enough for all in the café to hear, a Tyler's regular named Otis asked, "Hey, do ya'll know why them elephants out there painted their toe nails red?" For a moment there was silence before Otis shouted, "They wanted to hide from the Sheriff in a strawberry patch!" Everyone laughed, several slapping their knees and table tops.

"Yaw know why an elephant's foot is a sex organ?" a farmer in a John Deere cap asked when the laughter died down, "because if he steps on you you're fucked!"

Around the rest of the town, the ladies at Betty's Beauty Parlor were leaning out from underneath the egg shaped hair dryers to hear Betty's account of the hysterical situation; Little league ball players set aside their bubble gum baseball card trading at Cowlings Corner Grocery to read the newspaper's headline in the rack; and retirees playing dominoes on the first floor of the court house were reminiscing about the day long ago when a lion had escaped from another of the city's wintering circuses. In the later case, it was apprehended in less than a day near the football stadium. They all agreed that several days of elephants on the loose didn't carry near the impact of that lion running free through the town.

The phone, setting on Post's weathered wooden roll top desk, rang as he was sitting down to put his feet up. He answered with a matter of fact tone, "Post."

"Jeff, are you trying to start a stampede?"

"Hi Walter."

White had returned to his downtown office momentarily to check on business when he heard about the newspaper's unauthorized reward story. He wasn't happy.

"What do you mean by stampede?" Post asked.

"We have enough problems to deal with out there without having half of the people in this county running up and down the damn roads, making noise and getting in the way!"

"The more eyeballs the better I would say," Post countered.

"Did you have to offer a reward? If you would have checked with me first, we could have asked for volunteers to sign up at the Chamber."

"Just try..." White shut Post off.

"We've got an organized effort of volunteers and law enforcement going on and now we have to deal with a bunch of bounty hunters!"

"A hundred and fifty dollars is hardly a bounty Walter. Besides, it was intended to motivate people who live in the area to keep their eyes peeled."

"Maybe so, but we've already had people almost git run over by all of the people flooding in to take a look. They're stacked on top of each other like cord wood out there."

"Alright Walter, calm down, I'll squeeze something in this afternoon's edition telling them to be aware of the official posses and volunteers and to keep out of the way. Okay?"

"Even if they spot them how are they going to communicate it with us?" White went on. "Without the proper equipment they're just a bunch of loose cannons."

"Alright Walter, you've made your point."

"Let's hope we won't need to worry about your retraction but if we do, let people know that several of the roads where we're working will be shut off," White instructed. "And cancel the reward offer."

Post had just what he was hoping for; the newspapers were flying off the counters! Now if this thing could last for a few more days...

CHAPTER TWENTY-ONE

Burke had more on his mind than the additional chaos that Post's reward had created. While he drove his truck east along Coker Road, near Messer Point, he was thinking how improbable it was that someone other than Leon Johnson had not encountered Lily and Isa *somewhere*. Of course, someone actually had. Roland Hill, who could have easily handed them over to the authorities days ago and didn't.

He had chosen his present route in order to explore the two square mile area centered by Messer Point and bounded on the north and south sides by arms of the lake. Two additional square miles lay to the west and he would canvass that area as well later in the day.

Scanning both sides of the road with equal intensity, he reached the intersection, turning right on Rainey Road, going toward the lake's northern most side. Only a moment had passed when he spotted a 20 foot section of mangled fence wire and wooden poles. He slowly rolled his truck to a stop on the gravel, took a 360 degree look around while sitting in the cab, then pushed the door slightly open to avoid the squeaking sound it usually made. Once he was near the fence, he stepped over it into the high weeds to have a closer look.

"Bingo!" he said silently to himself, immediately recognizing that no ordinary herd of cows or deer could have left the welded wire fence in such a twisted mess. The deer would have simply jumped it. Cows would have stretched the wires apart and wiggled through it. Other than Sasquatch, there was no other explanation.

After several more yards of following the trampled grass came the first proof the elephants had been there, a very *large* pile of fibrous looking manure lying on the ground as if it had been twirled from an industrial size soft serve dispenser.

When it came to the process of evidence gathering, Burke knew never to assume. He smiled as that particular thought entered his mind, but, based upon the sheer size of the pile he allowed himself to *assume* he was at least looking at 30 pounds of elephant shit.

Still standing, he inspected the lower portions of several trees. Bark had been rubbed off in swatches and the markings led him to a shallow acre size swamp about 40 yards away. The marsh was a quagmire of dead tree limbs, soggy brush and rife with water bugs darting along the dark surface. Flies were whizzing back and forth on a line between the stagnant water and the smorgasbord left by the elephants. He was waving at a red wasp hovering close to his head as he was trying to stand still, listening quietly for nearby sounds of rustling.

There was little doubt left the elephants were on a collision course with the lake, granting Burke some relief considering the mountain strewn northern option they could have chosen.

He waited to contact the RV command post, choosing to do it from inside his truck to avoid being heard, although he was certain they had already picked up his scent. He gave Mullin coordinates to work with based upon the new information. They could now forego the south side of the giant cove that was Messer point and concentrate on the north side of the lake, which would be a considerable savings in time and effort.

CHAPTER TWENTY-TWO

It would take a couple of hours for the vans, horse trailers, pickups and RV to relocate at the corner of Griffin and Messer Roads near Highway 93. Meanwhile, Burke continued to weave his way further into the heavily wooded brush looking for an exact direction they could have gone.

Mullin arrived alone, fifteen minutes after Burke reported his whereabouts. He peered into the woods from his truck for a couple of minutes before rolling down the window and calling out for him. Hearing no reply, he placed his hand on the steering wheel to honk and then thought better of it. He finally exited the vehicle, closed the door quietly and walked to the fence line.

The odor reminded Mullin of the stench around the feedlot on Fridays at the sale barn. He gripped his nostrils with his thumb and index finger and in a voice an octave lower than normal yelled, "Damn Burke, are you dead in there? Geezus!"

"Not yet," Burke replied, curling underneath draping tree vines as he walked out of the woods toward him.

"Any sign of 'em?"

"Lots of'em," Burke said, "But they didn't stick around."

"You smell that? I'd git the hell outta here too."

"I gotta think they're at the lake right now," Burke surmised. "Probably spraying themselves off and feeling a lot cooler than we are."

White was delighted to have the trailer parked near Burgers, Beer and Bait, also known as Killer B's, a landmark watering hole known as much for the giant silver minnow spinning in the wind on the roof as it was for the amount of spinning heads the patrons usually left with. To his way of thinking, they were back in *civilization,* the RV would no longer be necessary. Killer B's was now the new command post.

He had quickly completed his task of having the flyers printed at Baldwin's Office Supply in Hugo. The four scout packs passing them out were promised a citation for their community service and each would receive a gold felt arrowhead to sew under the Bear patch on their uniforms.

A new sense of optimism prevailed. For the 11 men left in the posse, just the feeling of knowing they had a firm direction energized them. They were certain they could find and bring them home today. By being in a more populated area, the chances would be greater that they could get additional reports from someone nearby.

The flyer was helping, and the *hotline* was ringing with a couple of sightings. One had them due north and west of the area where Burke found the droppings and another had them south and west.

The distance in between the two was peculiar to Rose at the command post, but all had to be checked out. He summoned Curly to leave the tractor and trailer near 93 where it was staged and lent her his jeep to check the south sighting out. Burke was in pursuit of the north sighting. The posse was somewhere in the middle and pushing on west toward the lake.

One of the callers was a home-alone teenager with a mop of unruly brown hair and the other, a thin elderly woman wearing only a pink tee shirt, no bra and soiled blue pants. After face to face meetings with each, it was determined both sightings were false and probably made up with the hope of nailing the $150 from the newspaper if they happened to be caught in their vicinity.

After hearing that, White started to pick up the phone and give Post another piece of his mind but backed off.

Chapter Twenty-Three

The third phone call turned out to be the most plausible sighting for the moment, even though it was more *audible* than visual.

An unemployed used car salesman and his buddy, an off duty service station attendant, had been looking around most of the afternoon at the lake, and had agreed to split the reward $75 a piece.

They filled a 32 quart Coleman cooler with ice and two six packs of Coors, then trolled their dented and scraped aluminum john boat with a tiny two blade trolling motor around in the slews, going in and out of coves, until they heard vocal noises of what sounded like elephants.

"Shhhh! Listen!" whispered the car dealer, who went by the name of Sweet Pete, sticking his finger vertical to his lips. "Those are elephints ain't they?"

"I don't knooow. I ain't never heard no elephunt," answered Jackie, at 22 years old, a full 20 years younger than his friend.

"Well that sounded like one to me."

"I guess so Sweet," Jackie said, still not sure.

They set their beer cans on top of the ice chest, pulled the boat up to the shoreline and observed what appeared to be smashed grass and leaning in the direction of the sounds they heard.

"I think it was one'a them baby elephints cryin' for its mommy," Sweet said, still whispering.

Excited and not wanting to scare the elephants off before they could claim credit for their capture, they tip toed back to the boat, pushed it out as far as it would go without turning on the motor, then headed across the lake to the Hugo State Park Marina three miles south. At seven miles per hour it was going to take a while.

When they arrived, they hurriedly tied the boat off, ran inside and used the marina's phone to call the hotline from the number they found on the flyer posted to the door. In order to add some gravity to the situation, they added that they had caught a brief glimpse of the creatures.

After receiving word of the sighting, Burke, who had just rejoined the posse, quickly hopped into the Jeep that Rose and Wheeler had arrived in.

They drove at twice the posted 35 miles per hour speed limit, before parking as close as they could to the area of the lake that Sweet Deal Pete had described. After a half hour of searching the dense bottomland hardwood and wading around in the cove, they neither *saw* nor *heard* anything that looked or sounded like an elephant. However, they did determine there had been some presence of the elephants around there at some point.

Walking into Killer B's, the Sheriff said, "Nothin'," before anyone had a chance to ask.

"I didn't think you were havin' any luck when I didn't hear from you on the radio," said White. "Who called that in Burke?"

"Sweet Pete and Jackie from the Apco," answered the Sheriff, not having to use last names since everyone *knew* who Sweet Pete and Jackie were.

The posse, taking up all of the barstools after knocking off for the day, began laughing.

"What's so funny?" Burke asked looking at them confused.

White pointed over to a booth in the corner where Sweet and Jackie were sprawled out asleep, one on each side. "If those two were hearing or seeing something you'd have to search inside their heads for it."

Burke walked over and kicked Jackie on the bottom of his boot without getting any kind of reaction.

Jeff Post walked in as Burke was standing over the drunks. "I don't think those are the two that got away Sheriff!" The comment brought more rounds of laughs.

Post had heard the news about Burke locating a trail and arrived to gather notes for his next story.

"Pay'em Jeff!" Burke fired back. "These are the kinds of idiots that reward of yours brought out."

"There's a lonely old lady and a pimple faced kid that want their cut too!"

CHAPTER TWENTY-FOUR

RUSSIANS AND AMERICANS GREET EACH OTHER IN SPACE!

The interstellar event headlined the Tuesday morning edition of *The Daily Oklahoman,* the state's largest newspaper in Oklahoma City, accompanied by a large photo of former astronaut and native Oklahoman Thomas P. Stafford proclaiming it "The Dawn of a New Era."

The dawn of the fifth day since the elusive elephants fled into the forest of southeast Oklahoma garnered a bit of news itself, meriting a short report in the newspaper's *Oklahoma Beat* column on page five. Within the two paragraphs was a paraphrased statement of reassurance from Sheriff Blakemore that the truant pachyderms presented only a threat to themselves and none to society. He expressed optimism for a speedy recovery and made mention of the phone number for the hotline.

Burke, Wade and Chuck spent much of the morning on a pontoon boat provided by the U.S. Army Corps of Engineers, following the long shoreline and going in and out of crescent shaped coves. On numerous occasions they stepped onto the sandy banks and limestone landings to check marshes, exposed tree roots and bushes for signs of wallowing or foraging.

The posse, led by J.D. Little, was spread out two miles wide north to south and working their way east toward the lake. White, Rose and Curly continued to hold vigil at Killer B's, the RV now abandoned in the gravel parking lot.

After several hours of no luck in the coves, they steered the pontoon toward a string of random islands dotting the north side of the lake. With less shelter from the sun on the open water, they each took turns applying sunscreen, the hot breeze created by the speed of the boat feeling like an electric hair dryer aimed at their faces.

Within thirty minutes of island hopping, the new direction paid its first dividend. On a small, acre and a half sized island heavily covered in brush, only 30 yards off the lake's west shoreline, they spotted unmistakable traces of the elephants in the form of droppings and gigantic footprints on the narrow sandy shore. *Elephant Shangri-la,* the metaphor Rose had used to describe the protected wildlife and waterfowl refuge area on the north end of the lake, was a mere three miles away.

He notified the command post to alert the posse to vacate the woods and take a faster track on the road toward their location. Secondly, he said to alert the Pushmataha County authorities to have constables and marshals be on the lookout around the areas of Oleta and Rattan, small towns near the northern end of the lake. Rose, not wanting to involve additional authorities in the hunt as of yet, argued for a few moments about the second request but relented quickly when Burke suggested they needed him to round up several more private citizens to seal off the exit points as much a possible.

Burke jumped into the two foot deep water, sat down in it for a moment to cool off then waded along the shore inspecting the brush more closely.

"They were all over this place!" he half shouted as he spotted one indication after another where they had been stripping leaves and wallowing.

He confirmed Little's location then instructed him to have the posse meet them near the base of the Highway 93 Bridge. With Wade taking the pontoon to the bridge, Burke and Chuck would follow as much of the trail as they could, which would begin where the elephants had slipped out of the water and back into the woods. Burke and Chuck trudged the half mile of soggy bottom in 15 minutes, stopping only to untangle vines wrapped around their wet pant legs and muddy boots. The trail was still clearly evident, emerging a half mile south of the bridge. Not wishing to go any further until help arrived, they sat in the shade, waiting twenty minutes for the posse.

Resting on the ground, their backs against a couple of shade trees, Burke was enjoying the respite, "Those clouds need to stay there,' he said, watching them gather in a thick mass around the sun.

"I heard on the radio we may get some rain tonight," Chuck mentioned, "Maybe a thunderstorm or two."

"Another good reason to get this thing over with,"

"Well it'd be nice if it'd cool things down."

"We could use the rain," Burke replied.

Indeed, the cloud cover rolling in was helping. The scorching sun continued to have a detrimental effect on the search, cutting most days short for the riders and their exhausted horses. These were pretty tough guys and quitting wasn't in their vocabulary, but they had to protect their mounts, they had no choice.

CHAPTER TWENTY-FIVE

Curly pulled to the shoulder of Highway 93 with a horse trailer carrying two horses for Burke and Chuck, allowed them to climb into the cab and then continued driving to the base of the bridge.

The riders fanned out on each side of the highway south of the mile long concrete bridge, which was as much viaduct as bridge, crossing various points of the wild landscape when it wasn't over water. Some were looking for new tracks, and others like Burke and his group, were following in the direction they suspected the elephants were headed.

He knew what the elephants already knew about them, they were close by.

For Lily and Isa, the memories of confinement, enduring bull hooks pierced behind their ears and servitude were still fresh. However, that was then and this is now.

No one at the circus could have imagined the paradigm shift they were experiencing, the result of their new way of life. After several days of gorging on berries, sweet grass, fresh leaves and occasional melons, life was getting better and better for them. They certainly weren't behaving as if they were lost, the characterization their owner preferred.

They had proven to be highly stealth-like if necessary. After those first few hours of wandering the woods preoccupied with their new surroundings, they had acclimated purely out of necessity. They were past the point of fear and insecurity, the two things that Rose said would have them eventually trumpeting for help. This theory, along with all of the others he had, wasn't holding water.

What was holding water at present were Lily and Isa's trunks, joyfully braving the heat by spraying cooing jets over their humped backs while standing two feet deep in the lake.

The playing quickly turned serious when they heard the sound of hooves snapping twigs and the strong scent of humans permeating their nostrils. They began to fidget, turning to look in all directions, and then as the sounds grew louder, the fidgeting gave way to agitation. Their instincts took over, first suspecting that it could be predators. Elephants have no natural predators, but tame ones don't know that. Danger abounds for young elephants their size if it's a pride of lions, but this was Oklahoma, not Africa or India!

It was time to move. They exited the water, taking off in a north and easterly direction, further away from their pursuers. Unwittingly, the direction they headed was going to be trouble, an area where they could easily be boxed in.

Lily and Isa were capable of walking up long gradual inclines but were not steep climbers, so the elevated highway to their west with a sheer levee wrapping around to the northeast of them was a problem. The lake widened on their east side to the point that a swim, if it became necessary to avoid capture, would be out of the question. That left them few, if any, alternatives and the horsemen were moving in rapidly from the south following the substantial trail markings.

The compacted area lacked adequate places to hide and to turn around now would only take them back toward their *attackers*. For all intents and purposes, it looked as if Lily and Isa were out of options. Their freedom, their great adventure and new way of life was in jeopardy.

Standing in the wide open, their backs to the lake, they appeared in full view for the posse. Upon seeing them, Burke gave an order to stop, the eleven men now only a quarter of a mile away.

Following his direction, they created a 150 yard wide line, standing side by side, "We'll close rank the closer we git," he instructed the two horsemen on each side of him. They began passing it along to avoid having to scream it.

"Surround them but keep your distance."

Prior to the order to move in, Burke radioed the command post for Curly to bring the truck to the same area of the bridge where she had dropped off their horses. Two Highway Patrol units were dispatched to block north and south traffic on the highway. He suggested to White and Rose to enlist anyone they could to bring their vehicles to the bridge to help form a barrier.

Once they had the elephants surrounded, the scared pair was expected to cooperate fully with Chuck taking charge and then Oklahoma's first ever *elephant drive* would proceed. Grabbing hold of that thought, Mullin blurted out, "I bet the drovers on the Chisholm Trail never seen nothing' like this boys!"

Burke made a clicking sound with his tongue pressed against the roof of his mouth and shook the reins slightly for his horse to move. There was a chorus of more clicking sounds and the final march was on.

The dark clouds from earlier had been replaced by an even thicker wall of charcoal gray ones and a light rain began to fall. The temperature change was refreshing, with several of the riders tilting their heads back to let the rain coat their faces while others leaned forward to rub the water into the short hair on their horse's thick necks.

As the rain quickly picked up in intensity, they were undeterred. The water had begun dripping from the brims of their hats. Their gait was steady and deliberate, the posse staying tight with one another. With the rain turning to a downpour, compromising their field of view, they declined the temptation to speed up, the footing in the field limiting their options as it became more treacherous.

CLAP! CRAAAACCCKKK! A bolt of cloud to ground lightning suddenly hit close by, rumbling as if it were an echo for several seconds afterward. Two of the horses reared and several others joined them with each additional crack. They began to drift, no longer following their rider's attempts to control them. The riders fought to secure them, trying in vain to get them back on the track that was taking them toward the huddled elephants, themselves frightened to the point of paralysis.

Most of the soaked horsemen had never ridden in such conditions, and several chose to dismount and walk beside their horses. A couple of others stopped underneath a convenient clump of trees, knowing better, but doing it anyway. Burke, Mullin, Wheeler and two others remained in their saddles, riding side-by-side fifty feet wide, pushing ahead on pure adrenalin.

They rode toward the lake shore, still fighting the torrents of rain, and dodging scores of two and three feet high oak seedlings, seeing but ignoring the bolts of lightning hitting the lake in the distance.

"Call Curly and tell her to bring us a storm cellar when she brings the van," Mullin joked in-between lightning bolts.

Burke looked back, making an arm wave to the cautious riders of the group to get back on their horses and join them. Two of the men remounted and rode briskly to catch up.

The elephants were circling around each other in what looked to be a rain dance but wasn't anything of the sort. They were becoming more and more agitated by the powerful noise the storm was producing.

As the riders neared, they switched from their preoccupation with the storm to the commotion of the horses battling toward them through the soaked grass and seedlings. They began to back away, keeping a watchful eye on their pursuers, before Lily orchestrated a 180 degree turnabout to face the lake with Isa following suit.

Burke saw no avenue for an escape. They couldn't swim for it. Even if they decided to turn and charge the riders themselves, there were more riders positioned behind them to head them off. They would follow them all the way into the water if they had too. They had them! He was beginning to taste it!

CRACK! CRAAACK! CRAAAAAAAAAACCCKK! THUMP! At that moment, the straight line wind that had picked up to gusts of 60 miles per hour snapped a dead 90 foot tall cedar tree, the fall line crossing directly into the path of the riders. Mullin and Wheeler were closest to it, the limbs grazing them, but they narrowly escaped injury or even death.

"Everybody okay?!" Burke screamed, trying to ignore the panic he suddenly felt.

"Damn, can I get somebody to at least yell Timber!" Mullin screamed. No one laughed.

Mullin had hopped off his horse, trying to calm him down while grabbing the bit on Chuck's horse to hold him steady." Let's go, we're alright," Mullin said squinting up through the rain at Burke

Burke backed his horse into a turnabout and once he faced the lake again, he saw the elephants swimming toward the other side. He galloped toward the water, splashing into it several feet before stopping. He turned to the others on the bank, pointing out toward the water with his left arm.

"There's a sand bar out there they can climb out on!" he shouted.

They had managed to find a portion of water where a narrow strip jutted out into the lake. There was no way that the riders could have spotted it from their vantage point. It was far enough away that it originally gave the elephants pause before attempting to swim for it. However, desperate elephants make desperate moves.

He could see additional strips arranged several yards apart in the distance beyond the one they were on, all of them created by the drought conditions that had recently lowered the lake level. They could crawl out and rest momentarily on each, then finish their marathon to a far away bank on the northeast side.

Mullin rode up to Burke in the water. "So much for the lake being an obstacle for them," he said, "They'll be on the other side of the county in a few minutes."

Burke sat on his horse marveling at the two swimming swiftly and efficiently side by side, the tips of their trunks lifted above the surface of the water to breathe. He looked up at the rain, now beginning to ease, then looked past the elephants to get an idea where they were headed. In a straight line, they only had to make it three-quarters of a mile. By horseback, the same point was 5 to 6 miles away and there were no straight lines.

Lily and Isa felt the bottom beneath their hooves and walked to shore, exiting into the dense forest of the Hugo Lake Wildlife and Waterfowl Management Area, an inappropriately named area for the reason that, there wasn't really much *management* of a human nature. It was actually an anarchy and habitat where wildlife could roam free from hunters, highways and *posses*.

CHAPTER TWENTY-SIX

The following morning, the Sheriff's phones were ringing off the hook. The hotline, on the other hand, was dead.

The downpour aiding Lily and Isa's escape had not let up through the night, dropping seven inches of rain across eastern Oklahoma, pushing the Kiamichi River and its major tributaries, well beyond their banks, several of the roads and low water bridges were preventing passage with even more rain expected. Scores of residents had become stranded on the roads while even more were marooned in their homes. Out of desperation, many were putting themselves in danger by trying to cross the swift waters.

The electrical power was out in many areas, meaning water wells and septic tanks had ceased to function. Fortunately the cool front bringing the rain made the loss of air conditioning units tolerable, at least for the time being.

Being cut off from town meant losing access to necessary medical supplies, food and work. Being cut off from the post office meant having to wait on social security and welfare checks.

Crops of Alfalfa hay, wheat and soybeans yet to be harvested, lay drenched and with no let up in sight, would mostly be destroyed. On the other hand, some "farmers" in the more remote areas of the county would be happy that prominent weeds such as Rag, Chenopod and Nettle would flourish in the wet conditions. The county's third largest cash crop, *cannabis,* was a part of the moisture loving weed family too.

For emergency crews from the Hugo Fire Department, the Sheriff's office and the numerous volunteer fire departments from the rural townships, it was a busy day. The situation had quickly become critical but fortunately not dire.

It wasn't until early in the middle of the afternoon that Burke could spare an extra thought about the two elephants. Rose had waited until after lunch to call, registering concern about the cooling rains potentially energizing the elephants to roam even further into the woods, especially since the lake itself was no longer a barrier to migrating east.

With all of the distractions, Burke was uncharacteristically short with Rose, briefly describing what he had been dealing with since very early in the morning. The current need to prioritize, meaning putting human lives first and the elephant's lives second, was a hard pill for Rose to swallow. Burke didn't really care, and besides, he was reasonably sure there wouldn't be any elephants in the voting booths when he ran for re-election.

Rose, along with White and the others, had been busy relocating the command post location to the east side of the lake. White's suggestion to set up in the parking lot of the Dock "All You Can Eat" Catfish Restaurant and Bar near the dam in Sawyer was rejected for something a couple of miles further northeast.

With the flooding and mud hampering their efforts, they ditched the idea of moving around to the east side of the lake in favor of using four wheel drive pickups for canvassing along section lines, going door to door dropping off a few bags of groceries and asking for people to be on the lookout.

The impatient Rose returned to his office and again called Burke for a timetable to resume the hunt. Burke could only reassure him it would be soon, once the rains subsided, and only after everyone who needed their help was safe and sound.

After hanging up, Rose stood silently on his back porch, reaching for a cigarette pack on the table next to him but stopping short. He had promised his wife he'd quit. With all that had happened within the past couple of days, his confidence for a speedy recovery of the elephants had eroded significantly.

He pondered the idea that had come to him earlier in the day. After a couple of minutes, he reached for the cordless touch tone phone setting on the rail next to him and began to push buttons. While it was ringing on the other end, he lit a Marlboro.

CHAPTER TWENTY-SEVEN

The damp and soft forest floor was a welcome relief for Lily and Isa's nicked and scratched hooves. During each downpour, they stood in the open, washing and cooling their massive bodies while pushing the cool air over their backs by flapping their ears.

They began the day going back and forth around the edges of Apple Point on the northeast side of the lake, freely raiding the cantaloupe and honey dew melon patch belonging to Owen Williamson.

The rutted roads on which Williamson navigated his way to the fields were impassible and with the power to his TV and refrigerator still working, those were two good a reasons as any to take a little time off. Of course, he had no idea his field was under siege and wouldn't know for another day and a half.

The two napped while standing on a couple of occasions, letting the rain continue to cool them. They had zero motivation to go anywhere, choosing to remain near the bountiful food supply for the entire day.

During the night they dropped to their knees and rolled over on their sides, lying with their backs touching each other as the silent lightning in the distance illuminated the branches, creating the vision of shadowy stick creatures. They remained calm, and the previous experience from the night before, when they trotted in circles for hours terrified by the commotion in the sky had been a good teacher.

Tonight as they lied together, it was exhilarating. They would sleep until near dawn and see what wonders tomorrow would bring.

The dawn was wrapped in magnetic grey clouds making the seventh day of their freedom look much like the previous day.

With so much water everywhere, they were no longer inclined to follow the tips of their trunks as they had for the entire week. Instead, for breakfast they finished off the nearby cantaloupes before embarking on a slow sojourn due east.

The size of the elephants made blazing a trail easy. The soaked weeds and bushes offered much less resistance for their front tracks and their back tracks would quickly become a muddy bog, a prospect that wouldn't contribute much in the way of help when the search resumed. The closed roads remained free of passersby, making it easy for them to go across and walk along undetected.

The four wheel drive trucks offered a little opportunity to search in-between the section lines. The best Rose, Chuck and Curly could do was stop every half mile or so to wait and watch. Rose kept glancing at his two way radio under the dash as if he could visually make it ring with the good news of a spotting.

The three of them spread out, working their way south of where the elephants were last seen before their Houdini act. They were convinced the lake was still too strong an attraction for Lily and Isa to stray away from and they were at least partially correct. Lily and Isa were near a lake, but not *"the" lake*.

Schooler Lake was tiny by Hugo Lake standards, located two miles south of Spencerville near the northern boundary of the county, it comprised only 100 surface acres. It was surrounded by weekend cottages and a few residential homes tucked in among the verdant surroundings of weeping willows, elms and tall Loblolly pines. The main access to the lake was off of State Highway 147, a scenic two lane paved highway, which wound by tilled farms and cattle ranches before intersecting with State Highway 3 in southern Pushmataha County.

Lily and Isa wound up on the west side of the lake near its earthen dam, peering directly across at a row of small metal sheds and trailers resembling the caravan they once knew.

It was too close to people to even consider lingering for long. They were, however, further away from the posse than ever.

CHAPTER TWENTY-EIGHT

Burke was sitting at Best Café downtown, sipping a cup of paint brown coffee and reading the *Daily Oklahoman's* front page account of the elephant's harrowing escape and the subsequent floods ravaging the county. It was his first break since the rescue efforts had ground to a halt and his first venture into public since the search began.

The heavyset waitress with a gray beehive hairdo came over to warm his coffee. Burke put his hand over the top of his cup to stop her. "Hey Sheriff, you know why them two elephants crossed the road?" she asked.

His leer was meant to be audible then after a couple of seconds, he asked, "Why?"

"Because the chicken was tired!"

Even though Burke had heard that one more than a time or two he still tried to manage a smile. He had been losing some sleep over the situation but he had vowed to himself not to let it lose him any votes.

"Good one."

"I thought you'd like it," she said. "Pie?"

"No thanks, gotta take off."

He made a quick call to the office and was told that all of the residents that had been in peril were safe or had managed to move to higher ground. No one to their knowledge was hurt or still needed help.

After a phone call to the national weather service, he was assured the rain was coming to an end. At present, it was down to only a sprinkle and would end completely by evening.

Rose called for a third time to report their search had produced zilch and wanted to know when they would be back on track with the posse. Burke had already started the process of getting in touch with the horsemen and he promised Rose they would resume first thing in the morning.

Based upon Rose's group encountering zero leads along the east side of the lake, the new strategy would be to take a northern route, beginning on the east side of Highway 147, two miles north of Sawyer and three miles south of Schooler Lake.

The coordinates would place them near the center of an area that comprised 24 square miles. It would once again be like trying to find a needle in a haystack. A couple of long days lay ahead unless they were shortened by a confirmed sighting.

Burke was walking out of the café headed toward his car when he was met by two men, the older of the two introducing himself as Ron Higgins, a medium built man about sixty with a trimmed and oiled haircut which didn't give the appearance he was a local. The younger man with him, Wilson Williams, was taller and thinner, wearing starched Wrangler jeans, ropers and a blue shirt with pearl buttons.

"They told me at your office I might find you here Sheriff." Higgins said. "This fella here is Wilson. We're from Campbell's Soup."

Burke's blank expression turned to one of curiosity. "What is it I can do for you gentlemen, Mr. Higgins?"

"I'm here to inform you the cavalry's coming Sheriff!"

"Beg your pardon?"

"I'm joking...I'm president of the Campbell's Soup riding club and if it's okay with you, we're planning to bring our guys and gals over to join in the elephant hunt we've been hearing about!"

"Mr. Higgins, as much as I appreciate the offer, I think you folks may have the wrong notion of just what it is we're doing."

Higgins gestured with his hand as if to begin a reply but Burke kept talking, "From what I know about your group, ya'll ride in homecoming and rodeo parades, do trail rides and have picnics."

"Yes sir, we do but..." Higgins said before being interrupted again by Burke.

"This ain't a parade and it damn sure ain't a picnic."

"We think we know that Sheriff. Most everybody in the club is aware that the country over here is difficult to ride a horse through. Not that much different across the river in Lamar County."

"We're not new to this," added Wilson in a real Texas drawl. 'We've hunted hogs, coyotes, bobcats..."

"No elephants?" Burke joked.

"Not until now."

"We got a few who don't wanna ride with us but we got about 20 or so who will," Higgins said. 'It sounds like you need every hand you can get."

"You guys work in the soup factory huh?" asked Burke. The Campbell's Soup factory was huge, employing hundreds that lived all around Paris, Texas, a city of 28,000 and a shopping area for people in Choctaw County.

"Yes sir," replied Higgins. "I'm the General Manager and Wilson drives one of our trucks."

"I learned my alphabet eating that soup," Burke said almost wistfully.

"We make a lot more kinds than Alphabet Soup but I hear that from most," said Higgins.

"You gonna let all twenty of them riders off from work?" Burke asked.

"They work different shifts. They'll be here five to ten at a time."

"This is a once in lifetime opportunity Sheriff," Wilson added. "We run soup all day, can it, box it, truck it, go home, have dinner, watch *Mork and Mindy* on TV and then go back to work the next day..."

"Shoot Sheriff, my riders will take vacation time to get to do something like this!" Higgins said not letting Wilson finish.

Burke looked amused as he thought for a moment, then withdrew the toothpick he had been chewing on and pointed with it at the two, "Well I said this ain't no picnic and it ain't no vacation either Mr. Higgins."

"Just tell us where to be and when Sheriff. We got our saddlebags packed."

CHAPTER TWENTY-NINE

"WHAT'S HAPPENING HUGO!!!"

That was the rhetorical weekday sign on for Emily Bohannon and Jack Emory, local talk show hosts for radio station KIHN in Hugo. The popular pair had listeners tuning in throughout the day from their stores, offices, beauty shops, tractors, trucks and homes.

They called themselves A-EM and P-EM, Emily hosting the morning show until noon and Emory the afternoon show until six. However, during the rainy break in the hunt for the elephants, they convinced the station's owner to let them set up a remote studio at Hugo Lake State Park with the idea of co-hosting a show all day. Interest in the hunt had been growing rapidly with listeners ringing the station's phones off the hook wanting to hear more about it, and more specifically where they had been sighted recently and if the reward was still available.

For A-EM and P-EM, it was a potential ratings bonanza, the station upping its spot advertising rates 50% due to the larger audience. The two even set up their own hotline to take calls from listeners around the county who may have an idea on where to search.

For their first show, they began with a serious list for "What to do if you see an elephant in your yard." Eventually they jokingly gave tips on "How to actually catch an elephant that is in your yard."

The audience grabbed hold of the joke immediately with callers poking fun at the expense of just about everyone connected to the search. It was a nice reprieve for listeners mostly weary from the endless discussions about low grain and cattle prices and the post-Vietnam and Watergate years.

The crazy idea of two one ton elephants running amuck in a civilized area of the United States was becoming a sensation, one that was too much fun to resist by the national news networks. A-Em and P-Em spent their breaks doing phone interviews and were enlisted as phone-in correspondents for ABC, NBC and CBS.

Until the hunt was over, the two hosts were going to enjoy their 15 minutes of fame.

"Hello, and welcome to The Greatest *Radio* Show on Earth," Emory answered, playing off the circus's well known catch phrase. "And to whom am I speaking with?"

"My name's Janae Williamson."

"Hi Janae, are you calling because you've seen the elephants?" asked Emory.

"No, I haddint, but my husbun says he has."

"Where was he when he saw them Janae?" Emory asked looking over at Emily who sat listening through her headset.

"He said he saw somethin' had went to eatin' up his cantaloupes and honey dews. He figgered it wuz some deers or rabbits but dey wuz too minny of them dat wuz ate."

"Yeh, so he's certain it was the elephants?"

"Had to a bin," Janae quickly replied. "If them was rabbits that ate all them melons they'd hav'ta to be as big as them elephunts."

"Maybe the circus should think about putting those rabbits in their show," Emily said, still laughing.

"Somethin," said Janae, not really adding to the conversation.

"Okay Janae, let's give the Sheriff's posse and the Campbell's Soup riders some help. Tell us where you live hon?" Emory asked.

"We live on the road that goes out to Wilson Point but the lan' we got our mellins own is on the back side of the 40 akers."

"Alright Janae," Emily answered, "We're going to see if we can get in touch with Sheriff Blakemore and give him your information. I'm going to take you off the air and you give us your phone number, okay?"

"Okay."

"Alright folks, I doubt the Sheriff is listening in right now. If anybody out there near the Williamsons has seen the Sheriff close by, please tell him to call our hot-line at 555-Hugo."

"Janae," said Emory, "Thanks a bunch hon."

"Meanwhile, "Emory went on, "While we track down the Sheriff you can track us down at Hugo Lake State Park. Just turn right a mile past the entrance gate and we're at the end of Bobcat Road, sitting right here in the RV camp ground on a beautiful limestone bluff overlooking the lake.

Emily added, "The good folks from Sonic are here flipping hamburgers and serving Cherry Cokes so come on out for the trunk show!"

CHAPTER THIRTY

Willa Mae Robinson was placing the first of the hot apple pies she was baking on the window sill of the Virgil Baptist Church when she saw the dust from the Sheriff's truck as it blew by. "Now where's he goin' in such a rush," she said quietly although none of the other ladies in the church's kitchen heard her.

The ladies did hear the grinding and crunching sounds of the gravel from the second truck with the large trailer which had joined in the chase. Three of the ladies left their apple dicing and peach slicing to take a look out of the front door. "I wonder what all that fuss is about?" asked Margaret Hill, Roland's wife, as she placed the second of the hot apple pies on the sill to cool.

Burke glanced at the sign in front of the church advertising the senior luncheon and pie sale as he blew by. He allowed himself to muse just a little, hoping that a quick capture of the elephants at the Williamson's place would leave him time to return to the church for lunch and a piece of Willa Mae's blue ribbon apple pie.

Burke had KIHN turned up on the radio but was finding very little amusement from the radio host's attempts at humor. He turned north, traveling less than a mile east of the lake and two miles south of where the most recent evidence of the elephants had been found. He said a short prayer in his mind, asking God to let this be the day.

He and Chuck slid out of each side of the truck at the Williamson place, slamming the doors simultaneously.

Chuck took one step before turning around to reach through the window for his bull hook. Janae had paid no attention to their arrival, keeping her head down while sitting on the porch swing sewing on a pair of blue jeans.

"Mam, we had a call from the folks at the radio station that you all had the elephants we're searching for out here," Burke asked getting right to the point.

"My huzbun says so," replied Janae placing the jeans down in her lap. "Says dey ate up his melons and made a mess'a his patch."

Burke glanced behind the small white frame house and saw only a vegetable garden. Chuck walked around the other side and saw nothing even resembling a melon patch.

"Where bouts is your melon patch Mrs. Williamson?" Chuck asked.

"You can go round the house to a road you kin falla out. My huzbun's already gone to lookin' forim," Janae said while pointing in the direction of an empty car shed that set on the east side of the house.

Burke was turning to leave when Janae blurted, "what you gonna do with that thang?" pointing to the bull hook swinging in Chuck's hand.

Chuck didn't answer. Burke looked down at the weapon Chuck was brandishing and said, "Did you think you were going to need that to get them off her porch?"

"Habit Sheriff," Chuck replied.

"I think it'd be best you leave that in the truck until you need it," Burke said. "No one likes that thing!"

Rose and Wade rolled up in a pickup fully loaded with bales of sweet hay and ripe fruit. They had done their best to keep up with Burke but didn't want to lose any of the bed's contents. Curly sat in the road nearby with the engine of the tractor trailer idling.

Before Rose and Wade could get out of the cab, Burke was already behind the wheel of his truck. Without a word spoken, Rose backed out of the way to give him room to turn onto the still muddy lane behind the house and began to follow behind. Curly had nothing else she could do but wait.

Within a couple of minutes, the men were standing over the smashed melons and ripped up vines of Williamson's patch. There was no sign of Williamson except for his vintage looking green and yellow John Deere tractor parked near the carnage. Burke let out a sigh as he looked around and saw nothing indicating the elephants had decided to stay nearby.

"If he's out there thrashing around in those woods looking for them," Burke said referring to Williamson, "Then they won't be anywhere near here."

"Let's spread out," said Chuck, "see if we can find a trail that may at least indicate which direction they headed."

"This mud ain't helpin'," Burke replied looking down at a mish mash of tracks that were all running together and filled with the slime of crushed melons and water.

"It won't matter which direction because we have most of the riders coming up on the roads in every direction from here," said Rose.

CHAPTER THIRTY-ONE

The heightened anticipation of adding aerial assistance to aid in the search efforts had everyone from the Sheriff's department, the Chamber of Commerce, the Rose and Hahn circus and various members of the media gathered at the Hugo Municipal Airport awaiting the arrival of the Oklahoma Highway Patrol helicopter.

Rose paced back and forth outside the grey vinyl sided terminal building which sat on the end of a row of four metal hangars. Trying his best to calm his nerves, he asked Burke and several others to join him inside to discuss strategy for what to do once they have the elephants spotted from the sky.

As expected, most felt that once they have them sighted from the air, the chances were very high the elephants would disappear under the nearest canopy of trees, some so dense they covered hundreds of acres, where they could either change course or easily remain out of sight. The pilots would be instructed to hover overhead as long as necessary to observe the possible exit points if and when the elephants made an appearance. If there was no escape attempt, then the presumption would be they were now confined to a reasonably small area and the posse could move in accordingly.

It was actually more of an assumption thought Burke, but it was as good as any for now.

Rose reminded the group to not ignore any area, as the elephants had already proven they could evade capture by backtracking as well as ranging several miles in less than an hour when frightened. Again, everything that everyone already knew.

Since the pilots had to begin somewhere, the strategy would be for them to fly to the northeast side of the lake near the wildlife management area and stay on a straight line, north to south toward Highway 70. At that point, they would shift an equal distance east before going in the opposite direction much like the ordinary back and forth pattern one would utilize when mowing the front lawn.

Burke would review maps of the area with the two OHP pilots as well as the kinds of tell tale signs to look for in the high native grass and hardwood forests, such as foraging, downed fences, snapped trees or anything else resembling the progress of the two behemoths. Once they had visual contact, they would immediately notify the Sheriff who would, before dispatching the posse to a reported site, first have his staff check the current trails recorded to date in order to rule out previous markings.

Burke would also introduce the pilots to Lyle Crockett, the State Wildlife Manager for the region, who eagerly signed on to the team and Tommy Frazier, a sharp shooter with any kind of rifle including the tranquilizer kind. Frazier had traveled to Hugo as a favor to Ron Higgins, the Campbell's Soup man. He was a member of the Waco Riders, a small group in Waco, Texas that tracked and removed unwanted visitors of the varmint variety, sometimes using a tranquilizer gun if the rancher preferred to remove them peaceably. However, he was capable of administering a *permanent* solution if the landowner requested it.

CHAPTER THIRTY-TWO

Lily and Isa moved east of Schooler Lake, into an area bounded by meandering three mile stretches of dirt roads on the north, south, east and west. Their surroundings, equating to a sizable nine square miles, was similar to many of the others that had offered them food, shelter and rest. There was plenty of water in the narrow creeks and leafy low hanging leaves to strip, and although not their preference, they would do for now.

In order to cool off, they rolled in the shallow puddles that were spared from evaporation by the shade. Even if the puddles were black and tarry looking, their appearance made little difference to the two tired pachyderms, who joyfully lied down in them to take short naps.

Isa was up first, wondering about the trees, at times placing her trunk in the air to sense any presence of enemies. Just as importantly, she did it to ascertain if there may be more on their table tonight than the grass, leaves, roots and branches that had been sustaining them. Her instincts were constantly causing her to stop and listen for noises that could potentially indicate trouble. There was a distinctly different sound of something a great distance away. She wouldn't know until a little while later that the latest sound of trouble would be that of men and their machines.

Lily worked her way up from her side to her feet. Caked in mud, it was a reliable sunscreen that Isa had already coated herself with. Isa had circled back as if to say she had news of a place for lunch and Lily followed once her friend turned to go.

They walked purposely for a half mile, coming out from under the tree cover into a manmade clearing, where trees had been cut down and removed, comprising little more than one-sixteenth of a square mile.

The light was brilliant compared to where they had been, causing each to squint as they peered at row upon row of moist green leaves growing on hulking stalks of marijuana plants, some standing as high as six feet.

Still temporarily blinded, Isa stepped a couple of feet forward inadvertently stepping on and crushing a PVC tube that ran the length of the small field. Water instantly began gushing out around her feet. Without hesitation she lowered her trunk onto the broken pipe and began to drink as Lily immediately followed suit.

The pipes was positioned on each end of the field with additional rubber sprinkler hoses connected to the pipe and supported in midair by long steel stakes running between every other row. A large three inch wide hose was inserted into the end of each pipe and ran down a three foot embankment into a trickling creek. A structure, the size and shape of a medium size dog house was sitting along the edge of the bank protecting a porpane powered water pump which quite ingeniously facilitated the flow of water into the pipes. The conduits, once gorged with water, forced the hoses to provide mist to the plants.

Of course, all of this was lost on Lily and Isa. What was certain was that the fresh green delicious smelling leaves would be lunch and they would spend the next hour ripping them off their stalks and stuffing them into their stomachs.

The stalks towered over the two elephants as they each ate their way through a row. The ground was becoming soaked as they made no attempt to duck beneath the hanging hoses, ripping them from the poles. The spray of the water felt good, really good.

CRUNCH. CRUNCH. The leaves rustled as the limbs snapped back into place after being stripped clean. CRUNCH. CRUNCH. SLURP.

Within a hour, they were stoned. A little lightheaded but alert, they ventured away to find several vines of sweet blackberries growing on the side of the creek. Once they had consumed those, it was back to play in the mist and nap in the shade.

According to research on animal behavior, getting a buzz while grazing in the wild is nearly impossible to avoid. Many, such as deer, sheep and horses will seek out plants and roots harboring intoxicants and some may even have a drug of choice in some cases.

Perhaps that's why they chose to take a long afternoon nap before rising and rolling several more leaves into their trunks before they left.

CHAPTER THIRTY-THREE

The strobe effect of the whirling blades on the OHP helicopter could be sighted before the chopping sound of the engine could be heard. White was standing outside the command post near the lake talking to a couple of newspaper reporters when he saw the copter approaching, abruptly ending the interview to notify Rose and the others inside who were just breaking up another nauseating strategy session.

To some, like Chuck Wheeler, the Bell 47 helicopter looked identical to the one Alan Alda gazed out of each week during the opening credits of his favorite TV series M*A*S*H. The older White remembered seeing similar *whirlybirds* in person while in the Korean Conflict. For Rose, its sole purpose was to bring a swift ending to a darkly comical reality show that he had been living for nearly two weeks.

The copter landed softly on the tarmac about 100 feet from where 40 people were standing and Burke was the first to walk briskly toward it, keeping bent slightly and grasping the brim of his Resistol straw hat.

"Captain Morgan?" Burke said sticking out his hand.

"It's Mike, Sheriff."

Burke looked at his young co-pilot, waiting to be introduced.

"Bill Tangleman," said Morgan, as Tangleman walked around the nose of the aircraft.

"Hello Bill," Burke replied. "As I said on the phone, we sure appreciate you guys coming. To say the least we've been having a helleva time finding these elephants."

"It was pretty easy to see why when we were flying over," answered Bill, "Every little town we were seeing except Hugo looked like they had they had to bulldoze out some wide spots along the roads."

"Most of us have hunted and fished in these woods around here ever since we were kids and we know'em pretty well," Burke offered.

"I bet you weren't hunting elephants back then," Tangleman interrupted and smiled.

"We were all pretty confident we'd have these girls caught the first day, maybe two," said Burke, attempting to do a little face saving.

"I don't know much about elephants but I doubt they are as easy as coaxing a buck up to a salt lick and shooting him from a stand," said Bill.

"From the conversation we had Sheriff," said Morgan, getting back to business and walking in the direction of the waiting group of people, 'You have a trail established, right?"

"Correct."

"And so far, they hadn't given you any indication they have stopped or stalled their progress? They haven't actually confined themselves to any one area in the county?"

"So far, no."

"From what we could see on our topo map of the county, the area east of the lake doesn't have additional natural boundaries that could redirect them?" Morgan went on.

"We're pretty certain they would fear crossing the highway south of where we're standing, but I'm not inclined to rule out anything after this long."

Burke walked the two men over to Rose, White, Crockett and Frazier for introductions. "We're going to find your elephants for you Mr. Rose," Morgan said reassuringly.

"I don't have any doubt about that. I wish now we would have called you guys days ago. I never thought for a minute this could happen."

"Does this happen often, your animals escaping I mean? You guys have a lot of circuses I understand," asked Bill.

"We have four that winter around here," Rose replied.

"Five if you count the media circus!" White chimed in.

"We've had a few elephants get loose, a couple of tigers..." Rose said.

"Tigers!" Morgan exclaimed, glancing at Tangleman.

"Caught'em all in a few minutes without a big fuss," Rose said immediately.

"Good, I don't think I'd want to get close enough to nail one of those with my dart gun," Tangleman said.

"Dart gun? " Rose asked.

"I'm sorry Mr. Rose, we should be more sensitive. Rest assured if we have to tranquilize them it will be the best nap they've ever had. We won't hurt them."

"In the event we can get close enough, it may be that Lyle or I can drop, I mean tranquilize them, from the copter," said Tangleman. "We'll leave Mr. Frazier with you just in case you may need his help."

"And there's no chance my elephants can be hurt?"

"I've never had an animal yet that was, but the truth is, we don't really know," said Tangleman. "Larger animals can be a little more sensitive to the darts but the sedative we have loaded has been cleared by the FDA to not inflict permanent damage. Of course, we're talking about elephants here, the largest of all."

Rose turned to Crockett, the state wildlife department manager for Southeast Oklahoma had officially volunteered to help for the remainder of the search, "Is that what you have too?"

"Yes sir. I don't expect any problems Buster. Dr. Leonard gave us the antidotes in case they're necessary," referring to the local veterinarian that was a regular visitor to treat sick animals among the several circuses.

"I'll call him," said Rose. "He'll need to be ready just in case."

After agreeing to procedures for the ground crew, confirming coordinates and testing communication apparatus, Morgan and Tangleman lifted off heading east, coasting to the targeted starting point within minutes. Before beginning their southward pattern, they flew low along the edges of the beautiful new water impoundment, taking in the scenic limestone bluffs, the shimming water that mirrored the blue in the sky and buzzed the remote islands on the upper end.

While combing the first track of woods, Morgan relayed several spots where it was obvious the elephants had been but, according to maps, nothing that was considered new. They reported a busted fence which led to an assortment of tracks that at first appeared to be new until Burke revealed that it was he and his riders who had cut through the fence during their initial pursuit.

The copter drifted several miles toward the highway and began the second leg of the search, moving east then back north. The pilot notified Burke that everything below looked pretty much the same, suggesting they establish markers on the ground, perhaps posts with orange flags, to help keep their coverage unduplicated.

It was a slow track. Tangleman and Crockett kept their binoculars trained on the trees and especially areas of open ground beneath them which occasionally come into view. Morgan, although busy steering the aircraft, scoured the area inch by inch as well.

On the next turn southward, two miles due east of Spencerville, the copter would soon be flying directly over a massive grove of trees where, unbeknownst to them, two seriously stoned elephants were sleeping it off. Had Lily and Isa been of sound mind and body, they would have been spooked enough by the chopper's close proximity, no doubt running into full view and out of luck.

Tracks and markings around the Schooler Lake flyover gave the pilots a good indication they were getting closer to tracking the elephant's migration pattern. However, at present, they were no longer seeing any additional signs of movement, indicating they could very well have stopped to rest.

Morgan radioed to the search team to surround, as best they could, the area that was bounded by county roads E1990 and E2040 to the north and south and Tucker Road on the east, an area that covered 16,000 acres or 25 square miles.

As Burke jotted down the coordinates and instructions from Morgan, he turned to Rose and said, "Okay, so they've found the haystack. The hard part is finding two damn needles in it."

CHAPTER THIRTY-FOUR

Daylight was fading to the point that Morgan and Tangleman could no longer see clearly. After more than eight hours in the air including the flight from Oklahoma City, the pilots radioed Burke they would abort for the day and return in the morning. Morgan turned the copter sharply to the west and put it on a course for the Hugo airport.

For a day that had begun with the bright promise of help via the air, it managed to once again end in frustration. What made matters even worse, the people left in the search team surrounding the targeted area had begun to dispense, leaving holes in the perimeter; the length of time the search had been going had inevitably began eroding available manpower. Volunteers had to go back to work, while others had simply grown tired. The Campbell's Soup riders weren't having as much fun as they had thought with over half cutting their *vacations* short to return home. With only five or six riders actually on the payroll, there simply weren't enough numbers to cover the vast amount of area that needed to be searched.

Burke shared his concerns with Rose during the evening's post-search session, suggesting. "A more professional presence of experienced trackers under these conditions would be helpful." Rose agreed to speak with Frazier about the possibility of the Waco Riders joining the team, for a fee of course.

Fearing the elephants may leave the area they were assumed to be in, Rose instructed the remaining circus staff, which consisted of five people, to slowly drive the roads until as late in the evening as possible.

Meanwhile, daylight had faded quite some time ago for Lily and Isa. They had managed to slumber through chopper blades hovering overhead, dream delusional through the clopping and snorting of horses on the roads nearby and even sleep through a visit from four feral hogs that sniffed them before moving on to a more edible food supply.

The late afternoon hallways of the courthouse were filled with people, some in handcuffs awaiting charges to be filed, others speaking quietly with their attorneys. A few more sat alone or sprawled out, sleeping with their heads resting on the back of chairs.

Deputy Mullin had left the search a few days before to manage the Sheriff's office while Burke was leading the search efforts. "Welcome back stranger! Mullin bellowed when he saw him walk in.

"Looks like business is booming around here," Burke said while leaning back in his chair and placing his mud caked boots on top of the desk.

Darlene, another of the office's assistants, saw Burke glance at the thick stack of yellow call back memos, "Those are from a whole bunch of reporters and Mrs. Hunter called and wanted you to know that her ex was still stalking her.

"Did you have Wayne speak to the reporters?"

"They only wanted to speak with you."

"Too bad. If they call back, tell'm I'm too busy and if they want something to write about then they'll just have to come see for themselves. Let's not waste anymore time on interviews until after the search is over and the circus has them back."

He pulled the phone near and immediately began dialing the Hunter residence without looking at the note,

"Hello."

"Molly, everything okay?"

"Burke, John's been back for the last couple of days," Molly said with concern clearly showing in her voice. "He's parking near the house and just sits there like he's done before."

"All day?"

"Most of it. He just sits there drinking beer and watching. I can hear it every time he throws one of those cans in the back of his truck."

"Well at least he's not littering."

'Funny."

"Has he tried to speak with you at all?"

"I think that's the worse part Burke, he just sits there staring and drinking. I don't know what he wants."

"Is he out there now?"

"No. But his cigarette butts are."

"I'd suggest you take your little girl and go stay with your mother. Give me a chance to speak with him again before he has a chance to do something he'll regret."

"I can't do that Burke. That's what he wants is to run me off. I'd have to shoot my way back in here."

"Okay, then have a friend come over and call me as soon as he makes any kind of threat or if you feel you're not safe Molly."

"Thanks Burke, I hated to bother you. I know you have quite a job on your hands chasing down those elephants," Molly said with a slight laugh.

"Don't worry about it. I'm supposed to be chasing down the bad guys and protecting people like you," Burke replied quickly. "I'm not sure herding elephants is in my job description."

After hanging up, he picked up the stack of calls and thumbed through them. He began reading them out loud, "*Oklahoma City Daily Oklahoman, Dallas Morning*

News, Paris News, Tulsa World, Arkansas Democrat, KFOR, KWTV, KOTV, who are they? WFAA, the *New York Times, Sports Illustrated...*"

"The *New York Times* and *Sports Illustrated?*" he said to Darlene not expecting a reply.

He looked through the comments Darlene left on the notes, scratching the top of his forehead although it didn't itch. All of the notes asked for a return phone call, which he knew wasn't going to happen, however, the notes from the *Times* and *Sports Illustrated* indicated they were considering sending reporters to Hugo.

"*The Noo York Times?*" Burke again said out loud. "*Sports Illustrated?*"

"What's Sports Illustrated?" asked Darlene.

"It's a weekly sports magazine."

"Is this a sports story?" Darlene asked innocently.

"I don't know what the hell they're thinking this is."

He stood up, put his hat on and looked Mullin's way, "What the hell do people in *Noo York* care about what's going on in Choctaw County?"

"Maybe they're just killin' time until football season," Mullin offered.

"Who was that you were interrogating when I came in?" Burke asked changing subjects.

"The guy robbed the Roundtree liquor store with a toy gun earlier this morning," Mullin said. "We picked him up down at Grant sitting in his mother's house. Dumb ass drives five miles down the road, puts on a mask, robs a liquor store he's been to a hundred times and then goes back home to watch The Price is Right."

"Was it a water pistol?" Burke asked.

"Yep. Thank God it wasn't loaded."

Burke was smiling as he picked up the phone and returned Rose's call.

"Buster."

"We may have a problem Sheriff,' Rose said immediately upon hearing Burke's voice. "Captain Morgan informed me they could only spend one more day on the search before needing to return to Oklahoma City."

"Why?"

"Some kind of required maintenance on the helicopter."

"Hopefully one more day is enough." Burke said. "Can they come back if we need'em again?"

"They don't know."

"What about Waco?"

"Three riders are on their way now. Supposed to be here in the morning. They ain't cheap!"

"You'll just have to raise your popcorn prices Buster."

With the diminishing group of volunteers and the abrupt loss of the helicopter, Burke suggested that the reward may be a better idea than he at first thought. Rose hung up, thought for a second, swallowed hard, and then called Jeff Post at the *Hugo Daily* in order to raise the total reward to $250.

CHAPTER THIRTY-FIVE

The long afternoon nap followed by another round of weed, water and berries led to a short night's sleep for Lily and Isa. Lily jerked awake when slivers of light from the full moon began piercing through the leaves and branches over head.

The low light made it difficult for her to spot her fellow fugitive slumbering several feet away. A quick case of nerves, caused by the sudden fear of being alone, made her bolt to her feet, gathering her feet under her as quick as she could.

Isa woke abruptly, her heart pounding from the sudden commotion. She looked up at her friend who was now standing over her. Once awake, she felt a stabbing pain where her back was lodged against the base of a large scrub oak tree. She had been leaning against the tree before passing out. Her skin now stung from the splintered clumps of bark which stripped away as she slid down it to the ground.

GLOMP! GLOMP! GLOMP! Lily carelessly began dropping her load, not even bothering to move to a more private spot. It was more than enough to get Isa moving, squeezing her eyes shut and turning away while attempting to rise to her feet.

The sudden lightheadedness from rising to her feet had her head spinning and the normally surefooted animal went tumbling sideways into Lily, the two looking like two small grey planets colliding, before crashing to the ground and rolling onto their backs.

The natural curl of their thin lips gave the appearance of silly smiles on their faces as they came to a stop. The resulting thuds from their fall would have been a dead give-a-way of their location had anyone been able to venture close by during the night.

The starving elephants need for food, or call it the "*munchies*," far exceeded their need for shelter. They slalomed between the trees for several hundred yards before their elevated trunks caught the scent of fresh corn. It was a scent they knew well and a dish that was fed to them by the bushels *back in the day*.

The quest for the corn field would take them further east toward Red Road. They plowed stridently through the high grass, coming in and out of the trees before emerging at the edge of 20 acres of field corn. The corn had been harvested only a couple of days prior but there were plenty of stalks strewn about with cobs still intact.

Elephants are legendary for their memories. Every image becomes indelible and permanent in their minds. They can remember voices and faces they had known from years before. They can easily recall most every detail of their experiences, especially those of the past two weeks. So, at this moment, it was rather shocking that Lily and Isa had forgotten they were still on the run, One of the effects of the use of marijuana can be short term memory loss, so perhaps that was it.

Leaving caution to the wind, the elephants would now be within easy view of anyone passing north or south on Red Road. At the very least, they would leave an obvious clue trail as to their whereabouts. They couldn't care less. They ate voraciously.

At first light, the pilots would soon find new trail markings to follow-up.

CHAPTER THIRTY-SIX

Harold Willows, an Assembly of God preacher without a church at the present time and his friend Austin Ellis, a local rancher, had been independently tracking Lily and Isa for four consecutive days. Each morning they loaded their horses into trailers and met wherever they had heard the elephants had left the most recent clues to their whereabouts.

The 48 year old Ellis was short and bowlegged, usually wearing Wrangler jeans that bunched up around his knees and a straw cowboy hat pulled down tight around his ears. He had a ruddy complexion from years of sitting on a tractor in the sun and a nose which rolled into his upper lip. His buddy Harold was in his early sixties, sporting a still strong and wiry six foot three frame. Together they could pass for a Wild West version of Mutt and Jeff.

The two of them had refused to ride with Burke's posse, preferring instead to strike out on their own in hopes of getting the reward. One night they had even pitched camp when they didn't want to let the trail get cold. Back in town, they told their stories at Best Café and were sought out for a couple of television interviews which provided the comic relief at the close of the evening newscasts.

On the morning of their fifth day day out on their personal mission, Harold and Austin were riding their horses slowly along Red Road with the reins wrapped loosely around their saddle horns. Riding south, each sipped on tin cups of steaming coffee while taking in the brilliant dawn to their east.

They were excited to have found some *secret* clues as they began their ride; grass that had been mashed down, tree scrapings and a busted barbed wire fence with small traces of blood on it. Of course, with the $250 now almost theirs, they preferred not to share any of their information with the Sheriff at the moment. Instead, they had hoped to capture the elephants themselves, a feat that would surely make them local heroes and gain even more media attention. Willows allowed himself to think the publicity they would receive for singlehandedly bringing the elephants in couldn't hurt his chances of landing another congregation.

Before entering into the search, both prided themselves on being good hunters. Willows had stalked hundreds of deer and varmints while Ellis had tracked down runaway horses and helped in the recovery of stolen cattle all his life. However, the long daily rides were becoming tiresome and had it not been for the most recent clues, the two were almost ready to give it up.

Lily and Isa worked their way steadily through the rows of corn, each going a separate way but staying close to the thickets, trees and brush that ran along the west edge of the field. To their delight, the field had a rolling irrigation rig that had left small tributaries of water, helping to wash down the dry corn.

Lily wandered out of Isa's sight a couple of times, prompting enough concern with Isa, that she raised her trunk and trumpeted, at first slightly and then louder as if she were the older sister telling the younger one to stay close.

It was the second trumpet that caused Willows and Ellis to sit straight up in their saddles with their heads on a swivel, scouring the nearby corn field where they were sure the noise had come from. Each tugged firmly on their reins, halting the horses abruptly, and leaving them standing with their ears pricked.

"Sounded like that came from the far side of the field," Willows whispered. The field was a long open strip, easily ten acres in length but only about three acres wide.

Without answering, Ellis began to dismount, causing the leather saddle to squeak as he slid off. Willows put his pointing finger to his lips to insure they both remain silent then quietly turned his horse around, moving onto the edge of the field which was not bounded by a fence. With reins in hand and his horse behind him, Ellis walked through the field, surveying it the entire time, before remounting. For the moment, the saddle strains from the long days were no longer a factor. They each could feel their hearts beating rapidly in their chests.

Willows walked his horse quietly with Ellis following a few feet behind. The rows near the road had yet to be cultivated, still standing six feet high and providing cover as they moved in-between. They stopped, waited and listened several times while attempting to peer through any gaps in the rows they could find. By the look on their faces, the two cowboys were all business. As far as they or anyone knew, no one had been close enough to the two elephants to see them since the failed roundup in the rain several days before.

In order to remain out of sight, they were bent forward at the waist with their heads resting against the necks of their horses, giving the appearance of a pair of Choctaw Indian buffalo hunters from the mid-1800s.

They cringed a little each time their horses brushed the long leaves of the corn stalks and sloshed through the soft mud. As likely as it was they were getting closer to Lily and Isa, it was equally as likely the elephant's keen hearing had picked up their movement by now and scampered away. That thought made little difference to them, they both knew their horses were capable of outrunning the elephants if they could just keep them in the field.

"Harold," Austin whispered, "do we have a plan?"

"I wanna see'em first," Harold whispered back.

After a few more seconds passed, Willows offered, "Rope'em maybe?"

"Are you crazy!" Austin said in a much louder whisper than the one before.

"Maybe we try to head and heal'em," Harold answered, referring to the cowboy practice of one roper looping the head of the animal while his partner swings behind, dropping a loop under one or both of the animal's back legs.

"We ain't got ropes strong enough for that!"

Austin pulled up, suggesting to Harold that one of them stay close by, and keep an eye out for which way they may wander, while the other rides back to the road and calls the Sheriff's office from a house nearby.

Willows continued to walk his horse across the field, thinking about Austin's idea. They reached a small clearing, sitting for less than sixty seconds, when they heard what sounded like branches being crunched no more than 100 feet away. Willows looked over to Austin who was pointing at the thick stand of trees to their right. A few yards inside them, they spotted two pairs of elephant hooves, then four pairs.

THUMP! THUMP! CRASH! In the blink of an eye, Isa came barreling out of the trees causing the snapping limbs to go airborne, a few flying so far they nearly hit Willows. She was headed on a direct path toward the cowboys with her trunk rose vertically, pulling up within a few feet of them before halting. Their horses whinnied and reared up simultaneously, dumping Austin to the ground, Willows managing to wrap his long legs around his and hang on.

Alarmed by the excited men and frantic horses, Isa took off into the field with Harold giving chase only yards behind her. Austin's horse was backing up and away from him as he ran to grab the loose reins and hold her.

As he remounted, he looked around for Lily in the thickets but saw nothing. He could see Harold had closed on Isa and quickly took a parallel direction to try and possibly corner her on the fence lining the back side of the field. He was silently praying she would become exhausted and finally relent.

Still at the west edge of the field, Lily came out of the thicket, using the distraction that Isa was providing to sneak back to the south edge, going along it to the east, intent on helping her friend.

Harold, still on Isa's heels, galloped his horse evenly alongside the frightened elephant, the two animals' backs approximately the same in height. He instinctively began to lean to his left as if he was going to grab her around the neck and bulldog her to the ground. He immediately thought better of it and chose instead to reach out and grab the top of Isa's left ear that was pinned back for less wind resistance. That was the first of several bad ideas. Isa simply flopped her ear forward thrusting it into the side of Harold's horse. The horse dug its front heels in attempting a quick turnout while Harold went flying off the horse, hanging momentarily to Isa's extended ear before quickly letting go and landing in the crushed stalks, rolling several feet and winding up in the mud.

Isa made it to the southeast corner of the fence where there was a pair of locked steel gates, connected on each side by a small fortress of steel posts. She was left with nowhere to turn, quickly choosing to put her rear against the fence as Austin rode up and stopped. He was face to face, anticipating her next direction as if he were cutting a calf from the herd. She stood silent, looking Austin's horse directly in the eye as if to say "help me."

Just as Austin had hoped, the elephant was exhausted and seemed to become almost submissive. He slowly dismounted, picked up several stalks of corn and walked up to her, his hand out.

Harold kept a distance after retrieving his riled up mount, saying in a soft voice just loud enough for Austin to hear "I'm going to call the Sheriff. You okay?"

Austin never looked back at him. He just waved a hand toward Harold to indicate, "Go, I'm good."

Harold walked his horse away slowly, looking around but not seeing Lily. He remounted and lightly galloped toward the road and in the direction of the white frame house he had seen about a quarter mile south.

Austin tried to speak in soothing tones while attempting to calm the skeptical pachyderm and after a couple of moments, managed to put his hand on the middle of her trunk, rubbing up and down on it. Isa was flapping her ears slowly to cool herself down, her posture finally becoming more relaxed. However, she kept her eyes trained on the corn field behind Austin.

After a few more seconds passed, Austin's horse began making throaty noises and he immediately knew what was coming before he even turned to look. Lily was standing no more than thirty feet away, staring at Austin, as if to say, drop your gun and put your hands up.

Isa remained almost still, looking at Lily the entire time as if to say, "If you give up, I give up."

Austin slowly reached down and picked up another clump of corn. He held them out to Lily but she didn't move. Instead she walked over to Austin's horse, placing her trunk on the saddle to sniff the leather, then wrapped it around the saddle's horn.

The smell of the leather must have triggered unpleasant memories of the oxen-like rings the elephants were sometimes rigged to as well as the endless days of having a saddle strapped to her back while lugging screaming kids around. Whatever it was, it was disturbing enough to cause her to try and strip the saddle off the horse's back with one quick jerk. The frightened horse bolted toward the road leaving Austin stranded and standing between the two elephants.

She moved a few feet closer to Austin, stretching her trunk out as if to take the fist full of corn he was offering. She could hear him desperately urging her to take it. In one swift and powerful move, she twisted the tip of her trunk around his wrist pulling him down to his knees and then to his stomach. Austin rolled to his back as she let loose of his wrist, his first thought being he was going to be crushed to death. He screamed "No, please, no, no!" and held his right hand up to indicate stop. He turned quickly to his side and began to crawl away quickly, trying to get to his knees but mostly pushing himself forward with his feet and slithering on his belly like a reptile.

Isa took two steps then picked up her gait until she was in a trot alongside Lily, crashing back into the thickets, leaving Austin sitting on the ground, leaning back on his hands while he watched them flee. As he stood, he brushed the dirt off his jeans then looked around for the water he must have crawled through before realizing he had peed his pants.

No one was home at the white house on Red Road. Harold knocked on the front and back door, then walked around shouting but to no avail.

As he came back around to the front yard, he heard the faint sound of the chopper's whirling blades. Relieved, he ran to the middle of the road, standing there vigorously waving his arms in a crossing fashion.

As they came around, the pilots made a sweep of the area looking for a place to land, taking several minutes to scope the area, including the nearby corn filed. Hovering over it, they saw ample signs of the elephant's presence as well as a short, burly looking cowboy sitting on his horse, looking up at them.

Tangleman had already radioed Burke and his posse, directing them to head east toward Red Road.

They hadn't caught so much as a glimpse of the two elephants but had a bird's eye view of two cowboys and a corn field that looked as if it had a maze in it constructed by aliens.

They landed the copter on the road near the white house at the same moment the Sheriff, Chuck and the others, along with Curly in the tractor trailer, were pulling up.

They gathered around Willows and Austin hanging on every word of their wild story. It hardly made sense to most of them that these guys were trying to bulldog an elephant riding horseback, which is how Austin framed it, and they roiled at Willow's description of being tossed from his horse like a rolled up newspaper. Austin omitted his being submissively drug to the ground and pissing his britches.

Curly told them she didn't believe a word of it. "Besides," she said, "you wasint supposed to chase'm, just come back and tell us their location. Nobody's gonna catch them elephants on horseback!"

The fact that someone had actually been close enough to see them gave Burke a bit of relief even if the stories were too outlandish to believe.

Tangleman volunteered to stay on the ground with his tranquilizer gun so Burke and Crockett could hop in with Morgan for a look around.

They lifted off and took a spin over the area, circling around two more times. The three of them remained silent, preferring to remain on the lookout.

Morgan was looking out over the dense vegetation stretching for miles beneath them, then turned to look at Burke, "I now know what you meant when you told me I could be within twenty feet of them out here and not see them."

CHAPTER THIRTY-SEVEN

Female elephants in the wild never leave their mothers, staying with her and their herds their entire lives. Elephants living in captivity live in fear their whole lives. Perhaps worse than the fear they endure, it is the longing from being separated and sold to zoos or other circuses.

It wouldn't be a surprise if resentment was the fuel for Lily and Isa's escape and current contentment with their methodical, day to day existence in the wild over their previous lives. It had become plan A and there was no plan B.

After the harrowing encounter with the two cowboys, the frantic pair remained in full stride, guided only by their instincts to survive, blasting through a thick forest of short and tall evergreens interlocked together as if they were a jig saw puzzle. The sound of the snorting horses and screaming cowboys still rang in Lily's ears as she drafted behind Isa headed for who knows where.

According to geometry, the closest distance between two points is a straight line and at their present rate of steam they would put the largest gap yet in-between them and their pursuers, still gathered at the point where they met on Red Road.

After 30 minutes of vigorous running, exhaustion began to set in with Isa, who slowed her pace to a more manageable trot. The distance covered, along with the thousands of acres of thick evergreens and unimproved country side, would turn out to be more than enough to keep them out of sight.

As their heart beats restored to a more normal pace and their breathing became less erratic, they began to relax, each standing near trees offering the largest surface of bark to rub against. Within minutes of securing their massive hooves in the dirt and soft pine needles beneath them, they fell off into a deep nap.

The chopper, with Burke and Crockett aboard, was airborne, but there was no telling which direction they should turn. They would just have to wait and watch.

They continued to make sweeps for a couple of hours before Morgan noticed his fuel gage indicated a need to return to the airport, effectively ending the two days the OHP had been able to spare the craft.

"Look Sheriff, we both know you guys are going to find those elephants," Morgan said as they flew over the south end of the lake toward Hugo.

"If not today, then tomorrow, the day after, maybe a week from now."

"No doubt in my mind," Crockett added, "An elephant that's spent his whole life in captivity can't survive in the wild. They'll give up at some point."

"That's reassuring," Burke replied.

"I don't mean they can't for the time being."

"I know what you mean," Burke said. "That's what worries me, how long can they survive?"

"It sounded like they have plenty left in the tank if we can believe those cowboys," Crockett said.

"It's like hunting down escaped convicts," Burke said. "They always think they can survive in the woods before they start getting thirsty, hungry and bug bit."

"All I'm saying is once they get too far out of their element, they'll eventually gravitate to whatever is familiar."

"You just made me think of something," Burke shot back. "The circus carries one of their mothers, Isa's I think?"

A few seconds passed and Crockett looked at Morgan waiting for more from Burke, "Okay, and...?"

"Maybe that's what we need to do," Burke said while in thought, "Get mama out here."

CHAPTER THIRTY-EIGHT

The news of the elephant's close encounter with the cowboys and subsequent escape left the beleaguered posse, volunteers and circus staff disheartened.

Members from the Hugo Horse Club as well as the Rodeo Association, who had spared so much of their time to post eight to ten hour days, gradually had to drop out.

As the days went on, the four circus office staffers and a groundskeeper, continued spending most of their time patrolling the roads and looking for new clues.

Curly had continued to drive from section to section each day, baiting areas with piles of sweet hay and fruit, charting where she was setting her "traps" and then checking them regularly like a fisherman running trot lines. So far, she had come up with nothing and making matters worse, people passing by were tossing the hay bales into their trucks to feed to their cattle.

Rose thought the Sheriff's suggestion, loosely chaining an older elephant in the woods near the point Lily and Isa were last seen, had merit. However, he cautioned it would take at least as much as a week before the schedule would allow them to transport her home and into place. Never-the-less, it was a chance worth taking with the expectation her wails from the loneliness of being trapped in the woods would lure her daughter home along with Lily.

Wade, already on location with the circus in Texas, and Curly were assigned the task of returning Juliet to Hugo as quickly as possible. The circus would be left with only three elephants for several of their upcoming performances, but the show would at least go on.

Frazier's Waco Riders were booked at present, pursuing packs of coyotes preying on a prominent poultry farmer's operation in South Texas. They wouldn't be available for several more days.

The three riders and their tracking dogs would command a hefty fee of $500 a day. With $40,000 worth of elephants at stake and a circus on the road that was soon to be down 50% of their star attractions, Rose had no other choice but to stroke a check and wait.

The pressing responsibilities of the Sheriff's department, having been put on hold for over a week, was enough to cause Burke to step aside for a few days himself. Besides, he could also use the rest.

The elephant's trail had grown cold. The search was at a virtual standstill. Buster Rose was at the point he could only hope for a sighting by someone, anyone! It was time to increase the reward to $500.

During the evening of day fifteen, the Waco Riders checked in for a strategy session at the Rose and Hahn grounds, where they would use the available beds in the dorm that normally housed circus hands during the winter. There were ample stalls for their horses.

The three blood hounds were amped up, nervously pacing their cages in anticipation of a chase. In order to be immersed in the scent, they were supplied with blankets from the two elephant's stalls to sleep on. They would be provided with several more artifacts containing the elephant's scent in the field the next morning.

Without the services of the OHP helicopter, the Campbell's Soup riders and most of the local horsemen, there were only three search parties left: Burke's part-time posse, Rose's crew and the Waco Riders. Each would be positioned at the points of a geographical triangle based upon sightings and markings where the elephants had created a pattern.

"This thing looks like a Chinese fire drill," Frazier said, once the map containing each sign of elephants was sprawled out in front of his riders.

Frazier suggested Burke and Rose's groups switch with the riders as often as necessary in order to introduce the dogs to unexplored areas.

Burke asked if they should hold off one more day until Wade arrived with Juliet, however his idea was quickly nixed by Rose, who reminded him he was being charged by the day. He was ready for the riders to begin earning their keep first thing in the morning.

After having mostly observed from the air and occasionally from the roads, Crockett would join Burke's posse. However, not suitably skilled on horseback, he would maintain vigilance on the closest roads to them from his white Ford Bronco. By maintaining flexibility, he could quickly assist the riders if they called. In other words, *have tranquilizer gun, will travel...*

The need to come out of hiding more than likely never crossed Lily and Isa's minds since they didn't realize they went. After waking, they wondered about each day eating what leaves they could find and drinking from puddles and creeks. Their Zen had returned.

Occasionally, they would remain alert to the sound of a train whistle or a tractor plowing a field or the squealing of truck tires in the distance, but none of the sounds appeared to pose any real threat.

The minimal amount of food and water available was enough reason to continue moving on. Utilizing their wondrous *windows on the world,* they aimed their trunks in all four directions, determining a southeast route held the most potential.

By midnight, the three quarter sized moon granted enough stripes of illumination to walk along in the nearly pitch dark woods.

Dictated by the resistance posed by the path they were on, they had gravitated almost due south feeling at times as if they were back inside cages, the enormous scrub oak trees and impenetrable piles of brush keeping them closed in.

Not stopping to rest, they emerged in an open area with a very long and wide trail running east and west. The pebbled surface of the trail glistened in the light of the moon, specked, and giving the appearance of water droplets. Looking both ways, there was no end to the clearing in sight. After the jungle they had just endured, they couldn't wait to follow it out, needing only to smash the barbed wire standing in their way. It gave way easily from one mighty shove of Lily's right leg. Their efforts had paid off, and the way ahead would provide their smoothest sailing since the journey began. Isa stepped up to the edge.

After again looking both ways, she set her right front hoof on top of the hard surface, immediately drawing it back. Lily was already standing next to her.

The vibration her foot had felt was replaced by a low humming sound that was quickly becoming louder and turning into a familiar roar. Within seconds they spotted two large lights topping the hill less than a half mile to their west. Lily took little time in stepping back through the fence opening she had just created with Isa following swiftly behind her. A drifting formation of clouds blocked the moon's glow and the two behemoths, standing in the wide open, had managed to remain undetected as a pickup truck pulling an empty horse trailer passed headed east toward Fort Towson. After crossing scores of county and farm roads they had finally reached Highway 70.

For several minutes they retreated further into the shadows, watching one then two and then a third set of lights zoom by. With each passing vehicle they became more fearful, the whine of the engines and the squeal of the tires a reminder of the long and uncomfortable rides they once had to endure.

There was no turning back. The courageous effort they had made to get this far would have to be continued even at the point of exhaustion and starvation, which was setting in more and more by the second. Once again, they stepped through the fence opening, but this time there wasn't a moment to lose. They hustled up the slight embankment between them and the surfaced shoulder of the highway. They went directly across crashing through the two weathered rails of the wooden fence on the other side. Running without so much as looking in either direction, they found refuge among a clump of trees located a half mile south of the highway.

Relying upon their recent experience of having traversed thickly wooded areas, they came to yet another wire fence, Isa pushing through it without hesitation. This time they were stopped on the other side by a steep earthen wall.

The railroad tracks crossing through the middle of the county sat on a levee rising ten feet with a 30% grade, steep but still manageable. On the other side of the tracks, the levee slanted at the same degree toward more of the dense dark woods.

The track at the top of the levee offered another endless path free of obstacles, a prospect that greatly appealed to the tired animals. They easily climbed to the top of the levee, looking at miles of moonlit track to their east and west. More importantly, there was a very prominent smell of water not so far away.

CHAPTER THIRTY-NINE

Hugh Hutchinson had his freight train rolling 30 miles an hour, headed west. He would like to have been pushing it a little faster, but the deteriorating conditions of the track dictated his speed.

Every other day his freight cars were loaded with both finished and raw materials, mined in Southwest Arkansas and Southeast Oklahoma, headed for stops in Idabel, Hugo, Durant and Ardmore before turning around and heading back to repeat the process all over again. The railroad preferred the late night routes to avoid having to shut down to a crawl though the communities along the route.

Having just passed Fort Towson, 14 miles east of Hugo, headed west, Hutchinson was unknowingly on a collision course with two elephants currently following the smell of water in Lake Raymond Gary, less than two miles behind him.

Hutchinson blew his whistle several times as required when approaching crossings. In relation to the myriad of other more sinister sounds they had been hearing of late, the train's low lonesome whistle caused no immediate alarm. It was the much louder second, third and fourth blasts that stopped them in their tracks.

If there was indeed danger ahead, there was a problem. The levee had become elevated to over 15 feet high, dropping at a 45 degree angle on each side of them. The next sound of the whistle and beam of light about a mile ahead left them little time to think and even less time to act.

Hutchinson only had to control the speed of the engine as there was little need to navigate. The train moved effortlessly over the tracks. He had made himself a comfortable spot on the double wide padded seat, slowed to 15 mph to negotiate a long curve and because he didn't really have too at the moment, wasn't paying close attention to what was ahead. There was the occasional coyote or deer that was caught in the headlights but Hutchinson seldom noticed until he spotted them plastered to the front of the engine.

He was back on straight away track, prompting him to stand up and open the throttle. As he grabbed the top of the handle attached to the floor, he could see silhouettes of two very large objects on the track ahead, his headlights not yet able to pick them up.

He jerked back on the throttle, abruptly slowing the train and in doing so, he lurched forward and then fell backwards to the floor throwing his oft ailing back into spasms. The train was creaking slowly to a stop as Hutchinson fought gamely through the pain trying to stand up.

Lily and Isa had abandoned their shuffling, instead standing paralyzed in the middle of the track as so many animals do when caught in the headlights and confronted with a split decision. The sound of the train grinding to a halt brought them back to their senses. They forcefully turned around and bounded several feet over the ties before jumping the rail just as the slowly rolling train came to a stop a few yards past where they had been stalled seconds ago. They slid and tumbled into the deep ravine at the bottom of the levee, confusion and fear causing them to shriek and grunt, before winding up on their sides, too dazed to move. It would take a few minutes for them to determine if they were dead or alive.

Hutchinson, holding his back firmly with both hands, looked forward and then to each side of the levee. The immobilized elephants were lying in the darkness and he neither saw nor heard anything. Unable to see all the way to the bottom of the levee he had to leave it be, whatever *it* was. His ailing back would not allow him to step down from the train and he knew he'd never be able to climb back in.

He limped slowly to his seat next to the throttle, pushed it forward and reached into the compartment in front of him for a half empty bottle of Tvarski's vodka. He took one pull and then another, set the bottle between his legs and soon the train was rolling again toward Hugo. He knew he'd need to buy another bottle in Ardmore for the trip home.

CHAPTER FORTY

With the sun rising and quickly warming the morning air into a convection oven, the dogs were turned loose in the cornfield along Red Road. Finally released from the pen, they scampered helter-skelter, grabbing scents, running in and out of the rows, along the fence line and back into the trees until their noses guided them up a trail west of the field and through the thickets.

Frazier and his three riders, their horses still in the trailer, remained near the truck drinking coffee and dipping Copenhagen while listening to the dogs. Their nonchalance was a concern to Rose standing beside them, but Frazier assured him their approach shouldn't be mistaken for indifference. They knew the kinds of whelping sounds the dogs would make if they came upon something, even being able to discern if *something* was something other than an elephant, such as a raccoon, armadillo or wild boar. The latter caused the most concern, having had a few of their valuable animals maimed or killed in past encounters with a boar attempting to defend himself from the pack.

"I would expect the fuss those dogs are making would make my elephants run even deeper into the woods Tom," Rose said while pitching the cold coffee out of his cup in order to pour another.

"Let'em." Frazier replied. "Once they have that scent they won't stop until they catch up to them. There's no way those blimps could out run'em."

The speed of the hounds coupled with the imposing terrain made attempts to follow the dogs for any length of time impossible. While walking with Rose to have a look around in the field, Frazier compared hunting with bloodhounds to hunting with Blue Tic hounds, better known as coon dogs, which typically gave chase to a raccoon for many miles until treeing it.

Frazier first felt the bug for tracking animals when coon hunting as a boy in central Texas with his father and uncle. Coon hunting was a common, often hilarious and somewhat cruel pastime in the rural South. Several trained hounds were set loose while the hunting party usually sat around a late night campfire drinking beer and playing poker. Talking and listening as the dogs became more distant, they waited patiently for the barking to turn to a chorus of high-pitched yelps indicating they had one "treed."

Once it was time for the men to begin walking or riding horses or ATVs toward the barking, the dogs would be rewarded with the raccoon. The real *fun* was actually how the dogs would get the raccoon, who usually sat high in the tree on a shaky branch hoping to scare the dogs away by snarling his teeth and making low growling noises.

The hunting party would form a circle around the base of the tree shining flashlights on the raccoon as one of the men scaled up its side, stepping along the sturdiest branches available until he could reach the 'coon. Usually this task was performed by someone new to the hunt or perhaps by the one who simply possessed the most bravado. With a few violent shakes of the limb, the raccoon would generally lose its balance, gliding head first to the ground and into the waiting pack of vicious dogs.

It wasn't a sport for the faint of heart nor was it a particularly productive one. The truth be told, it was a way for guys to get out of the house and drink beer with their buddies while waiting for deer season. In Frazier's case, it was early training for a 20 year long career as an expert animal tracker.

The bloodhounds were swiftly putting a sizable distance between themselves and the riders. Once Frazier reached the fence line to the west, he froze when seeing the dogs had actually exited where the elephants had entered the field. In other words, the dogs were *back tracking* the elephants. With one hard silent blow on his dog whistle, the dogs reversed course, streaking back toward the cornfield.

He walked around to the south end of the field as he waited on the dogs to return. While standing beside the downed fence posts where Lily and Isa had drew away from their two would-be elephant wrestlers, the dogs raced past him, going through the proper opening into the woods and leaping the fallen timber and sniffing each tree and bush the elephants had brushed against.

Rose gambled on the elephants circling around and gravitating back toward the lake. With the dogs hot on their trail, he instructed Burke to post three of his posse west of Red Road and the other three, led by Chuck, east near Tram Road, in case they continued toward the mountains to the north.

No one gave any serious thought to posting along Highway 70, clinging to their earlier theories that the open surroundings on each side of the busy road as well as the constant traffic would keep them heading in any direction but there. The thinking was, if they did go south, crossing the road or pacing alongside it, it would certainly catch somebody's attention.

It was the dogs that would soon prove their theory wrong. They were snorting and barking furiously around the area where the elephants had busted the fence and held their ground the previous night prior to making the perilous crossing over the highway.

The revelation would turn the entire operation on its ear. With Highway 70 now the northern boundary,

Burke and Rose revised the search area as they drove toward the new meeting site, plotting the Kiamichi River as the western most boundary, the Red River to the south and Lake Raymond Gary to the east.

If the elephants remained on a southern track, they would be less than nine miles from the Red River and Texas.

"We may need fins and snorkels pretty soon," Frazier joked to the riders. He gave two silent blasts from his whistle cuing the dogs to halt and wait to be kenneled.

From viewing the map of the county's southeast portion, Frazier knew any of the water crossings named would deaden the scent for his dogs. If the elephants were to swim across the Red River, Texas would be a totally new ballgame. Time was of the essence.

CHAPTER FORTY-ONE

Still dazed, confused and sporting several sore muscles, Lily and Isa walked gingerly along the trench beneath the levee. They were nearing Fort Towson, a community of 700 people, the east side of which sat on the banks of Lake Raymond Gary. Named after a former Governor of Oklahoma, the narrow three mile long by a half mile wide lake with a state park attached was home to several dozen private residences surrounding its scenic shoreline.

The rails crossed by bridge over the north end of the lake. On their present course, their track would take them through the sparsely populated south side of town and directly to the lake.

As they approached the city limits, the noises from the town didn't deter them. Tired, sore and hungry, they simply no longer cared. In their present state, an encounter with humans may be just what the doctor ordered.

Only a few mostly deserted streets were in the vicinity of the abandoned Fort Towson depot, no longer necessary once Hugo usurped Fort Towson as the county's most prominent trade center in the 1920s. Few, if any of the people living nearby were home. If they were, they were in front of their room air conditioner, paying zero attention to what was just outside their windows.

Occasionally they heard voices when passing the wood framed shacks and trailers, most with front porches serving as storage for most of their resident's worldly possessions.

Near the end of their short trek though the town, a three year old blonde headed boy with dirt smudged on his left cheek and bare legs, walked onto the porch of one of the shacks, letting the wood framed screen door clap shut. The boy began searching through the messy piles looking for a toy, not looking anywhere else at the moment. His mother called to him to come back inside and as he stood to turn around he saw them. He expressed no real surprise, only boy-like wonder at the sight, staring for several seconds and cocking his head to one side as if deep in thought. He knew from Saturday morning cartoons what elephants looked like.

"Mama! Mama! Ella phunts! Mama, mama!," he kept screaming as he pulled open the screen door running back inside.

"Tommy, I'll go out there on the porch and help you look for your elephant as soon as I get this pot roast in the oven," she answered. "Now go wash up. Go on!!

"Mama! Ella phuants!" he shouted again, imploring her to come and see while tugging on her apron.

"Honey, I told you I'd help you find it in justa few minits."

Frustrated, he stood there without leaving her side, waiting for his mother to finish. She continued to slice the carrots and celery while watching Truth or Consequences on the black and white television setting in the living room.

Tommy couldn't wait any longer, bolting toward the front door, pushing it open so hard it slammed against the outside wall of the house. By now the elephants were nearly out of sight, a loud slap of the door connecting with wood putting more pep in their weary steps. Within seconds they were concealed in the grove of trees standing between them and Tommy.

Tommy's mother came walking through the door, wiping her hands on her apron and in a stern voice said "Tommy, what's got into you?"

"There wuz ella phunts Mama! Look!" he said loudly, pointing toward the grove of trees.

"If they're here they'll be over here sweetheart," she said as she bent over the pile. "We'll find somethin' for you to play with."

Tommy kept pointing and looking in the direction of where the elephants were headed. His mother continued to search through the piles not paying any attention.

"Mama, down there," he said still pointing.

"If it's here we'll find it hon," never once looking at him.

CHAPTER FORTY-TWO

With the fresh scent and new trail reported, Burke was eager to stay on the search, but had other law enforcement duties to attend to first.

At present, he was headed toward the west edge of Hugo where a filing station had been robbed and its owner shot in the leg while giving chase to the lone robber.

He notified Rose and asked him to notify Frazier, Crockett and Chuck about his need to chase a two-legged fugitive instead of the four-legged kind.

Frazier's riders unloaded their still saddled horses, mounted and began to ride east along the railroad tracks where the dogs had picked up a strong scent.

With the dogs running alongside the levee and well ahead, he knew they shouldn't be too far behind the hulking targets. He eased a bit in the saddle knowing that a trip to Texas was most likely off the table for now. It was time to just let the dogs work.

The dogs surrounded the area where the elephants had recuperated during the night before, snorting, barking furiously and digging at the ground. Frazier and anther rider known as Jelly Bean, slid down the levee on their butts to get a closer look. It was obvious there had been some kind of accident. He inspected the skid marks and smashed weeds looking for signs of flesh or blood or both. There were no indications of cuts or scrapes, just plenty of rocks and stumps that could have likely caused a few serious bumps and bruises.

He looked up at the riders sitting on the tracks after spotting several large strips of dung covering the side of the levee all the way to the base. "I don't know what happened but whatever it was literally scared the shit out of'em!"

Jelly Bean, so short and round he about busted out of his shirt, reached into his pocket and popped a couple of purple jelly beans into his mouth. "They survived whatever it was."

"If that much crap came out of you Jelly there wouldn't be anything left of ya!"

It was pretty apparent that a fall from the levee by the usually graceful animals had to have been caused by an oncoming train. Frazier radioed the sheriff's department and asked them to check the schedules for any trains that had ran through Fort Towson in the previous 24 hours.

During the Waco Riders' stop to inspect the crash landing area, Lily and Isa, now feeling less groggy and stimulated by the smell of Lake Gary's fresh water, had began to pep up to a slight jog. An additional provocation was the smell of the dogs on their trail.

One of the many things that a varmint hunter like Frazier wasn't aware of regarding elephants was significant; an elephant's sense of smell is greater than even a blood hound.

CHAPTER FORTY-THREE

Nature is rife with oddities. One of the strangest of which is the swimming ability of a fruit fly, a small millimeter sized gnat, compared to that of an elephant's. One of nature's tiniest creatures on earth, fruit flies seem to survive forever whizzing around the bowl of fruit in kitchens, yet, when a glass of water is placed on a table, they will perform a suicide plunge. On the other hand, one of nature's largest creatures, the elephant, makes the mere act of walking look painful, yet can swim gracefully for miles without so much as touching bottom.

That ability emboldened Lily and Isa to step cautiously down the levee on the west end of the Lake Raymond Gary Bridge, effectively losing the fast closing Waco Riders and their dogs at the water's edge.

Still tired and sore, floating in the cool water renewed their energy and gave their aching feet a much needed break, However, they had little time to spare, the dogs barking sounded closer by the minute, They sloshed their way through thick growths of Cattails lining both sides of the lake and when pressed to leave their cover, they swam underneath the surface using the tips of their trunks as snorkels.

For the second time within the hour, they were again in view of any resident of the area, but thus far, none had caught their attention. Frankly, they were more concerned with ditching the dogs.

The riders remained near the west side of the lake, at times walking or riding in a circumference around the area. Knowing the elephants would have to come up for air as well as exit at some point, they maintained a constant vigil with their binoculars trained on the surface and across to the east side. The dogs were fixated on the portion near the reeds where the elephants had entered the water, a spot where a several feet wide portion of the shore was turned into a bog from the mud bath the two had enjoyed while coating their overheated skin.

Without a scent to follow, the dogs could do nothing but bark, sniff and await orders. The riders searched the area for several more minutes waiting to see where Lily and Isa may emerge. Frazier had a suspicion that they swam straight across the lake to the east and that once back on land would make it their mission to search for a meal. There was every reason to think, based upon the evidence at the base of the levee they had uncovered, that they would stay close to the lake while searching for their next food source.

Rose was at home in his office when Frazier radioed him.

"Apparently they are good swimmers." Frazier commented without offering any kind of greeting.

"They've proven that. Do you see them? Where are you?"

"Lake Gary, we tracked them down the railroad tracks to the northwest edge."

"Have you got'em!?"

"No, not yet, the dogs are off the scent. We aren't exactly sure which way they went when they swam across."

"They swam across? Again?"

"What else could they do? We're checking with people in the homes and cabins, hopefully they saw them."

"Hell, they may still be in the lake," Rose said.

"Maybe. But I seriously doubt it."

"We're on our way," Rose said, clicking his radio off.

The partly cloudy skies were darkening with thunder rumbling off in the distance. The rain began to fall lightly as Frazier and his three riders walked their horses toward a nearby home, settling in under a large car port to wait it out.

The men chatted and watched the rain intensify. All the while, there was a teenage boy bouncing on a trampoline in the side yard, never once acknowledging the four strange men and their horses huddling near them.

The boy's dad appeared a few moments later, a medium size man dressed in cut offs and a white tank top. Frazier introduced himself and told him why they had wound up under his roof. They talked for a couple of moments, Frazier watching the boy perform his flips in the rain, before he eventually asked, "How old is your boy?"

"13," said his dad. "He's constantly on that thing. Says he wants to join the circus."

"Mine's 14," Frazier said. "He don't have enough sense to come in out of the rain either."

A giant clap of thunder spooked the horses and the boy kept on doing flips, seemingly unfazed.

His dad laughed and said, "He's all boy."

The rain began to pelt the metal roof.

"So's mine."

"You know, when that boy was born," his dad began, "I wanted him to become President. Then he got to be 10 and I thought I at least wanted him to go to college. Now that he's 13, I just want him out of the damn house."

The quip brought a round of laughs and Frazier asked what the boy's name was.

"Phillip," his dad replied.

"Hey Phillip!" Frazier yelled. "Did you happen to see a couple of elephants go by while you been jumping on that thing?"

Phillip looked over at the men for the first time and stopped jumping. Hanging on the side of trampoline and placing his feet on the ground, he replied, "You're huntin' elephants in Oklahoma and I'm the one that don't have no sense?"

They were all still laughing as walked past them and into the house.

Rose found the riders in the rain about 25 minutes after leaving his house. Burke, Chuck and Crockett arrived about five minutes prior and were planning to patrol the roads along the east and west sides of the lake. The roads didn't intersect, instead forming two semi circles. The road on the east side of the lake continued south.

With only two pickups at their disposal, the riders climbed in the back of each. Crockett and Chuck went to the west side with Burke and Rose going along the east. Frazier and the riders penned the dogs inside the homeowner's cyclone fence and stayed on watch near the lake shore.

Rose instructed Curly to assist Frazier by bringing his truck and trailer to get the horses and dogs, then circle back with the big van.

The rain was coming down harder. It had been an usually wet July for Choctaw County. The humidity making the days feel hotter and the elephant's trail cooler.

Once Lily and Isa had made landfall, they crossed the road and headed through the trees, at times walking through herds of curious cows, and covering over three miles in the ninety minutes they were given while the searchers reorganized.

They had unknowingly confounded every theory any-one had about their expected direction. Whatever seemed the most obvious thing for them to do, they did the opposite. During their latest travels, they stopped along the way to strip three small Muscatine trees of their smoothly rounded red berries and drank fresh water from a nearby cattle tank, voraciously eating and drinking like a couple of longshoremen on payday.

Idling the trucks slowly along the roads, their eyes trained on both the surface of the lake and the surrounding woods, Chuck spotted Burke's headlights in his rear view mirror, pulling over as he pulled alongside. Rose's head was shaking no in anticipation of the obvious question.

The clouds had made it prematurely darker than normal and along with the drenching rain, there was little chance to locate any points of departure for the elephants. The lone dirt road that wound for several miles south of the lake had become impassable.

Burke stepped out of the truck, slamming the door shut. He adjusted his hat, pulled his collar around his neck and began walking down the road. The other three stayed put.

He walked for a quarter of mile, in and out of trees, before his extra effort paid off. He found an area where several small trees and brush piles had been tramped down.

"It looks like they're tracking east," he said returning to within ear shot of the group.

Surprised that Burke had spotted a route so quickly, Rose asked, "You have any idea where they could wind up from here?"

"I do."

"Where?" Rose asked.

"They could drift south to the Red River or they could stay due east and head into McCurtain County, both of which are appealing choices to them but not for us."

"Good Lord. There's maybe two roads in the area between here and McCurtain." Crockett lamented. "My dad always called it no man's land growing up."

"Yep." Burke added, distracted by his own thoughts.

"They used to mine down in the area," Crockett said, "Cut timber too."

"Those mining and logging roads will have been grown over a long time ago." Burke replied.

"I can try to get the chopper pilots back down here," Rose volunteered.

"And if you can't?" Crockett asked.

"Don't matter, we can't waste time waiting," Burke interrupted, "In the morning we put two men on each section and walk, ride, crawl, whatever we gotta do."

"And we'll have Wade chain Juliet near one of those roads at first light," Rose said. "I'll make sure to tell him he'll be spending the night out there with her."

"No hanky-panky," Frazier joked.

"There's nine of us," said Rose. "But you can't count on much from me, I'm too damn old."

"Tommy," Burke said, "Leave the dogs home. The place we're going will rip them a new asshole."

Lily and Isa's instincts and cunning had helped them finally find their way as far from their pursuers as they possibly could be. They had crossed N4930, the last road on the eastern side of the county. They had blasted through one final wire fence standing between them and open country. Had they been able to read the hand painted sign they passed, they would have known they were *hafway 2 hell.*

Chapter Forty-Four

"So let's begin with the most obvious question Sheriff, how have two elephants been able to outsmart and outlast so many people for the past several weeks?"

The gentleman asking the question was Jack Goldberg, a reporter from the *New York Times,* who had been seeing and hearing so much about the comically bizarre story that he had to come and see for himself what it was all about. After flying to Dallas and arriving in Hugo two days ago, he tracked down Burke in a booth at the Best Café.

Burke bristled, noticeably irritated by Goldberg's phrasing of the question.

"Mr. Goldberg, those elephants are lost in a heavily wooded area the size of some states up your way. You make it sound like they are playing a game of hide and seek."

"It's certainly fair to say they were lost the first few days but they're giving the appearance they now prefer it that way," Goldberg responded while writing a note on Burke's previous reply.

"Look Mr. Goldberg, they're tame elephants in unfamiliar territory. They're hungry, dazed, confused...every sound they hear makes'em fear for their lives. I'd call that lost. You seemed to think they are out on a bender."

"So you are saying they aren't making every attempt to avoid capture?'

"I'm ain't saying that at all. You are. I can't know what those animals are thinkin'. Hell if I could do that we'd had'em a long time ago!"

"Let me put it another way," Goldberg said, reshaping his question, "Do you think these elephants want to come home?"

"Mr. Goal burg," Burke said, this time dragging his name out while taking a moment to measure his reply, "They've been outside of captivity long enough for their instincts to completely take over. As I said, they're scared and they're driven by the need to keep finding the huge amounts of food and water their bodies need. That's what keeps them moving."

"Any idea where they are now? Are you getting closer to finding them?".

"Yep."

"Yep?" Goldberg repeated. "Does that mean you're confident you're close to capturing them?"

"Until you're there in those woods, you really have no idea of what I'm talkin' about." Burke huffed. "I'll tell you the same thang I told the copter pilots that were here. They could be standing 20 feet away from you and you couldn't see'em."

"Trust me Sheriff, I'm driven around for the last couple of days and I've seen the forest you're speaking of. The question is, has anyone that lives around the areas where they have left trails not seen them?"

"A few people, but it's an extremely dense part of the county they're in. Southeast Oklahoma is one of the most rural areas in the country. It isn't unusual for only one home to sit on two sections."

"Sections being square miles?"

"Yes."

Goldberg thought for a couple of seconds, "How may reporters have actually been here?"

"Not many. They want to call and ask questions."

"So you think if more would come to see for themselves they'd understand the situation you're in?"

"I don't have Hemingway's way with words Mr. Goldberg, ' Burke said.

"Hemingway? You read Hemingway?"

"Just becuz it's the country doesint mean we're stupid." Burke said as if disgusted.

"So what do you mean?" Goldberg asked.

"It's difficult for me to describe what we're dealin' with by talkin' on the phone."

"Well, I'm here Sheriff and I have a way with words."

"Why are you here? Does anybody in Noo York really care bout what's goin' on in southeast Oklahoma?"

"Sheriff, no doubt you're aware that Jimmy Hoffa came up missing last week."

"The big mafia guy they let out of prison?"

"Yes. A very significant story, especially in New York, the speculation is he's dead and his body dumped underneath a construction site."

"What's that have to do with this?"

"Those two elephants of yours are on the same front page with the Hoffa story."

Burke kept looking at Goldberg, holding his coffee cup just below his bottom lip.

"That's why I'm here Sheriff. People think this is a joke. They want to know how two elephants in Oklahoma of all places, can hide in plain sight."

"Plain sight?" Burke repeated his voice rising.

"People are curious to know why they don't stand out in a state known for farm animals and not wild animals."

Burke rubbed his face, his resignation beginning to show, "Plain sight?" Is that what you people really think?"

"That's exactly what most people think. People in the east still think people living in Oklahoma travel in wagons over rutted roads. They know very little about what goes on anywhere else but New York. I'm not being insulting and I'm not proud of the fact that so many are like that. Most have never even been outside of the city."

"Well I've never been to Noo York so you can figure what I think about that place without having seen it." Burke said, seeming more enlightened.

"I'm glad you understand."

"This whole county," Burke said, going to a new subject, "Actually, all of this part of Oklahoma, Northeast Texas and Southwest Arkansas have enough natural habitats for those elephants to survive for years. The problem is they don't know how because they're tame."

"Like the Serengeti?" Goldberg asked.

"You probly don't think I know what that is either but no, not like the Serengeti. The Serengeti is wide open. I think they call'em savannahs. There's not much like that in the area where these elephants are."

"I think those people in Noo York City watch too much TV," Burke went on. "They watch nonsense like Chester galloping his horse between skyscrapers and think that's the way it is."

"You mean Dennis Weaver in McCloud? He played Chester in Gunsmoke."

"They'd be better off watching reruns of Gunsmoke," Burke replied.

"You ever rode a horse Mr. Goldberg?" Burke asked while sliding out of the booth and standing up. "Gone anywhere besides Noo York?"

"I've been several places on assignment, all over the world Sheriff."

"Have you ever rode a horse?"

"Once or twice, yes. Even an elephant in India."

The waitress, standing behind the lunch counter, hollered to Burke that Walter White was on the phone.

"What, Walter?" asked Burke, standing at the end of a row of red vinyl stools.

"Burke, I have a couple of magazine reporters here to do a story on the elephants and I've told them about all I could tell them. It's a man and a woman from *Sports Illustrated* and he wants to go out in the posse with you."

"On a horse?"

"He says he knows how to ride." White answered.

"Really!" Burke glanced over at Goldberg, and then said, "Do they teach horseback riding in that Noo York reporter school?"

"What?" asked White, confused.

"Nothing. I'll get two more horses trailered. Pick Mr. Goldberg here up in front of the court house and bring them to Eugene Whitley's place."

"Blue Whitley! Is that where you're going?" White asked, his voice raising a little.

Burke hung up the phone and walked over to his booth, "Come on newspaper man. I have'a *assignment* for you.'

Except for the recent robbery attempt, when a local liquor store owner blew the holdup man through the plate glass window with his shotgun, the occasional moonshine bust was usually the biggest crime news emitting from Choctaw County. The fact that two reporters from *Sports Illustrated,* the popular weekly magazine that usually featured John Havlicek, Pete Rose or the Dallas Cowboys on the cover, were in town asking questions had elevated the community's interest levels to new heights.

Christy Tannehill, one of the reporters from *Sports Illustrated,* had spent two days tracking down as many people as she could find who were known to have had an encounter with the elephants. Some of the stories she heard were doosies, to say the least. In fact, separating fact from outright fiction was becoming less and less of a concern for Christy. She began to think, what would subscribers rather read, credible tales or colorful tales?

She had gathered plenty of material, beginning with the account of the story of the two elephant wrestling cowboys in the cornfield that had been flicked away like a cigarette butt. There were plenty of others, the two that gave chase by bass boat on the lake, *"Tarzan"* and Curly's initial search near the grounds and the Sheriff's posse that had them cornered, only to watch them dog paddle away in a raging thunderstorm.

She was as thorough as possible, tracking down and speaking with several of the volunteers, local riders, Campbell's soup employees and the riders from Waco. She attempted to nail down sources for the two most incredible stories floating around town; the elephants supposedly laying a giant moonshine still to waste and the demolition of a field of Marijuana stalks. However, Roland Hill walked her back to her car with a shotgun after she showed up on his porch and to no one's surprise, she could not associate a name with the ingeniously engineered cannabis patch.

While being escorted to her car, she asked Roland about the flattened wild boar found next to his place. He offered the only explanation he could think of, "it must have gotten caught under one of them space ships that's always landin' out in them fields."

The raided melon, berry and corn patch stories were so numerous that they paled in comparison to all the rest.

It wasn't until she heard Hugh Hutchison's very embellished account of his following close enough behind the elephants on the railroad track, "That I coulda grabbed their tails," that she knew she had about as much information as could be reasonably believed once the story was published.

She left town after hearing the elephants had left the bloodhounds howling on the shores of Lake Raymond

Gary, swimming to freedom once again. Unfortunately her deadline for the magazine was near and she had yet to have a conclusion for her story.

Phillip Allen Atwell, *Sports Illustrated's* associate editor covering the story with Christy, was sitting in the back seat of White's 1969 red and white Cadillac El Dorado convertible watching the dust of county road N4390 billowing up behind him. He was listening to White lament to Goldberg, seated in the back also, about the turmoil the elephants have been creating for the county's Chamber of Commerce. Rose was riding shotgun.

After spending most of the 45 minute drive *selling* as well as telling the two reporters about the county he was born and raised in, White said "we also have an election comin' up for a new Choctaw Indian Chief..."

"They still do that? Have a chief?" Goldberg interrupted.

"Well yeh, the Choctaw Nation has a chief. Who do you think runs it?"

"I didn't know there was another *nation* inside the United States that needed to be "run" as you describe it," said Goldberg.

"The capital is in Tuskahoma, in Pushmataha County. They got their own jurisdiction. Ever hear of the Treaty of Dancing Rabbit?"

"I'm almost afraid to ask," said Atwell, "what's Dancing Rabbit?"

"In the 1830s, the Choctaws signed a treaty with the United States to swap their native Choctaw Nation land in Mississippi for a larger amount of land in Indian Territory. That's what half of Oklahoma used to be before statehood."

"Every school kid knows about Indian Territory, the five civilized tribes and the Trail of Tears, Mr. White. I doubt they know that the tribes themselves are still organized and each have a Chief no less," remarked Atwell.

"Well that's just one of the things going on," White said moving on to the next subject in a free form of consciousness. "We have the largest Blue Grass Festival in the country right here in Choctaw County starting next week. They'll be 20,000 people here."

"Maybe they can help you find these elephants," Atwell said jokingly.

"You fellas ever heard any bluegrass music?" White asked.

"Violins, banjos, is that the music you mean?" Goldberg asked.

"Fiddles, violins are for you city boys. All-day long--fiddles, gittars, banjoes, people love it." White said. "You guys ought to stay around and do another story."

"That may be one for *Billboard* magazine. I'll be sure and suggest it." Goldberg said, trying to be smart.

"Be sure and tell'em there'll be barbecued armadillo, fried possum, snake steaks and even some rain dancing," White said, now having a little fun with the *foreigners.*

As White was rolling to a stop in front of Whitley's acreage, Atwell and Goldberg looked at one another after reading the red lettering streaked on the large hand painted sign near his gate stating *You R now hafway to Hell an this here is privit property. Trespassers wil be shot. Survivers wil be shot agin.*

White was clearly enjoying the moment when Burke leaned down over the two reporters in the back of the convertible and said, "Saddle up!"

CHAPTER FORTY-FIVE

The horses, saddled and shifting their weight from foot to foot, were waiting along the sandy road in front of Eugene Whitley's massive 20,000 acre farm. An area covering almost 30 square miles. Whitley's place was considered a farm for tax purposes but few really knew what actually went on there. The less than inviting *greeting* posted near the entrance certainly kept anyone from straying too close.

Whitley's home sat over a mile from the front gate. He didn't have a phone or possess a television for that matter, leaving Burke zero opportunity to announce his posse's presence in the immediate area. He had no choice but to clip the lock holding the chains around the posts and push open the thick metal gate.

The posse was down to eight: Burke, Chuck Wheeler, Lyle Crockett, Tommy Frazier, the two reporters and two of Frazier's riders, Ben Bob, a lanky weathered looking cowboy in dusters and a guy they called Cowboy, who looked less like one than Ben Bob. Rose, never able to spend much time outside during the heat of the day, returned to his office to run the touring circus's business by phone and White, who occasionally searched for the elephants on dirt bikes with his 13 year old son, made sure the guest reporters were taken care of before doing a turnabout and spinning up dust as he headed north away from them.

Crockett agreed to remain at the gate to wait on Wade, now back with Juliet, whom they hoped would attract Lily and Isa enough for them to allow themselves to be captured. Once he and Curly arrived with her, she would be staked out the on the far east side of Whitley's property.

Burke gave the order for riders up and watched as the two reporters exhibited no discernible skills for mounting and controlling their horses. Burke ambled his horse over, dismounted and then remounted as he instructed how to do so. After a couple of tries, they began to get the hang of it, finally relaxing and following the rest of the group through the gate.

There wasn't an actual road running to Whitley's home, only ruts carved from the repetitiveness of truck and tractor tires rolling through the featureless knee high Switch grass. The posse walked their horses slowly in single file, each slumping forward away from the direct sun, holding the reins lightly or crossing their arms over the saddle horn. The scene bore a resemblance to the Confederate soldiers that once camped at Fort Towson, before riding toward a nearby skirmish with the Yankees at the Battle of Boggy Depot.

In the lead was Burke, his .30-30 rifle securely fastened to his saddle, then Goldberg, Atwell and Frazier, with his .44 magnum holstered and tranquilizer gun strapped on his back. Ben Bob and Cowboy rode side by side, Chuck was in the rear, prepared as always with his bull hook in its scabbard.

"What's that for?" asked Goldberg as rode up alongside Burke, motioning toward his rifle.

"Bear, Wildcats, Rattlesnakes," Burke said never even looking at him and trying not to smile.

"We may see bears?!" Atwell said from behind.

"Don't be surprised."

"Have you ever shot one?" Goldberg asked.

"Never have. Black bears wander over her from Arkansas, sometimes they get this far."

"This place is quite a menagerie," Atwell said.

There's wild boar, bobcats. Any of'em will attack if you come between them and their young," Burke said as he pondered what a menagerie was. "You have a better chance of seeing Copperheads and Rattlesnakes."

"What's a managerie?" Frazier asked.

"Animals, a large variety of animals," Goldberg answered.

"Like you got in Noo York?"

"Ha! Probably more snakes than anything else," Goldberg said.

"We even pull a few gators out of the Cypress swamps and farm ponds around here sometimes," added Burke.

"Alligators? Isn't that more Florida and Louisiana?"

"They come up the Red River from Louzyana then they'll slip out of the river and into somebody's tank. They've been known to grab a heifer when she comes for a drink of water."

"A tank?" Atwell asked.

"A pond."

"You guys have your own language here Sheriff," Atwell said. "We need an interpreter."

"Just another way of life Mr. Atwell."

Atwell and Goldberg simultaneously looked beneath them, the possibility of rattlesnakes had their attention for the time being.

Eugene "Blue" Whitley was given his nickname after sneaking a six pack of Pabst Blue Ribbon beer into his locker in Jr. High School. He and two of his buddies were drunk on two beers each when they were caught peeping into the girl's dressing room before band practice. He was subsequently suspended from school for two weeks and never went back.

He had inherited the entire farm from his grandfather who grew it to its present size by buying acreages adjacent to it when it came up for sale.

His father had farmed it several years after his grand-father grew too old, but when Blue was a teenager, his father was bounced from the seat of his tractor while brush hogging clods of dirt, getting run over and sliced to pieces by its cone shaped blades. After that, Blue lost what little enthusiasm for farming he had, choosing instead to hunt, fish and tend to his stills and leafy stalks of marijuana. His moonshine was legendary with sales coming as far as 150 miles away. His pot, by Choctaw County standards, was the best you could get your hands on, pre-rolled and sold only in fat joints that he referred to as *pocket rockets.*

He was short with thin stringy blond hair sticking out of both sides of his green John Deere ball cap. He was stocky, two weeks overdue on shaving, every bit the red neck and proud of it.

The posse approached the front porch of the house from the west, the sun sizzling through the collars they had pulled up to protect the backs of their necks. The two reporters took the wet bandanas and caps offered by Ben Bob and Cowboy, wrapping the damp cloth around their necks and tugging the caps down tight just above their eye brows.

Dilapidated cars, trucks, pontoon boats, rusty sheds, ancient tractors and a couple of newer ones, were strewn end to end around the front and sides of the house, forming an eclectic fortress. Blue was known to trade his *merchandise* for vehicles, guns, knives, pumps, metal or anything else he could convert to cash. The seedy types knew he was good for whatever they stole and needed to fence.

Burke expected Blue to recognize him or at least his badge and spare them both the song and dance of looking at the business end of a rifle sticking out of his porch window. The bird dogs announced their arrival first, barking continuously once they caught their scent, prompting Junior "Sponge" Clemmons to walk around from the back of the house, wiping grease off his hands with a red rag.

Clemmons was a thin six-foot-two black man with a permanent bland expression on his face. He knew the Sheriff but didn't recognize any of the others, especially the odd looking guy in the cap and bandana wearing navy blue double knit slacks, brown penny loafers and white collared dress shirt.

"Sponge," Burke said, preferring to greet him using his name instead of hello.

Sponge spit and wiped the corner of his mouth with the rag, "What's got you all dis way down here Sheriff?"

"We're huntin' elephants Sponge. Have you heard we've bin trailin' a couple of elephants"

"No. I had no idea we even hadda season on'em," Sponge responded in a slow drawl causing the riders to laugh.

"Being in season never stopped you from huntin' anything has it Sponge?" the Sheriff shot back.

Sponge thought about it for a moment then let it go. "I guess you here lookin' fo' da boss man?"

"He around?"

"What fo?" asked Sponge.

"We just need his permission to ride around the place, look for tracks and markings. They broke through your fence along the road. We're fairly certain they're around in here somewhere."

After listening to the conversation between Sponge and the Sheriff from the open front door, Blue walked onto the porch with two Chihuahuas barking around his ankles. "Afternoon Sheriff," he said as he reached down to slap both of the dogs to shut them up.

"Blue, you got the place lookin good as always," Burke said smiling and looking around the junk yard.

Atwell and Goldberg were trying to conceal their astonishment as they peered around a place that looked very much like a metal grave yard.

"I been hearin' you ain't had no luck finding them elephants."

"We will."

"You think you gonna do it ridin' them horses around here with two bankers? They look like their butts is already sore." Indeed, Atwell and Goldberg were standing up with their feet in the stirrups to give their rear ends a break.

"You got a better idea?"

"You know good n' well you woodin' make it more than a half day ridin' them horses through these woods and down into them blowouts."

"We've made it okay. No worse for the wear," Burke said, knowing he was lying.

"There's false bottoms back in there, covered cliffs, them boys be fallin' off sideways, snap a neck."

The conversation went on for several more minutes, the riders asking questions about the terrain and any suggestions Blue may have for avoiding the dangers he'd posed.

After listening intently, Goldberg, sweating profusely, rode alongside Burke. "Sheriff, would it be too much trouble if I could get a ride back to town?"

"What's the problem?" Burke asked knowing the answer.

By now Goldberg had heard and seen enough. He climbed off his horse, his blue slacks shredded below each knee, handed Burke the reins and said, "Sheriff, I'm done. I think I'm going to go on back to New York and tell those people exactly why you can't find those elephants."

"Sponge," Burke said, "can you run Mr. Goldberg here back to the road?"

"I can if I kin git one of these cars started," Sponge said looking over at Blue.

"Use the tractor," Blue said.

Sponge fired up the tractor, clasped Goldberg's arm to pull him aboard and rolled out slowly over the ruts. Goldberg, standing straight up behind Sponge and holding on to his shoulders, never looked back.

Burke radioed Mullin to send a squad car to Whitley's, then watched with the others as Sponge took the deflated reporter to safety.

"You mind if we water our horses and rest them for a little bit Blue?" Burke asked.

"Buckits over next to that well," Blue said pointing at it about 20 yards away.

Burke climbed down, handing the stirrups for his and Goldberg's horse to Cowboy and Ben Bob.

"What's that I smell cooking?" he asked Blue.

"Possum and sweet potatoes."

"Possum?! You can eat those things?" Atwell asked.

"Tastes like chicken," Burke said.

"More like armadillo," Blue said.

"We appreciate you letting us come on your place and look around," Burke said sticking out his sweaty hand to shake Blue's dirty one. "You don't exactly have a reputation for welcoming guests."

"Did I have'a choice?"

Blue waited a few seconds, obviously thinking of what he wanted to say next. "I know them elephants is here Sheriff. I heard'em las night. They don't sound like nothin' we got round here at night."

"You're think they're very far away?"

"Don't know that. Can't say as to where they is now. But like I sed, you ain't gonna git to'em ridin' horses."

"You sayin' we walk?" Burke asked surprised.

"Come round here a minit."

Blue lead him around to the back of the house where at least a dozen donkeys were grazing in a field behind a wire fence.

"Mules?" Atwell uttered as he walked up behind them.

"Jackasses is whut we call'em," said Blue. "That's how you gonna find them elephunts down in those blowouts."

"What are blowouts?" asked Atwell.

"Abandoned limestone quarries," Burke answered. "They blew up the rock, crushed it and hauled it out of here by the trainload years ago."

"Now it's nothing but deep wide holes filled up with water," Blue added. "The big ones you kin see, the small ones covered over you havta watch for."

"Why jackasses?" Atwell asked.

"They're more sure footed," Burke replied.

"Are they broken?" Frazier asked, meaning have they been trained to carry riders.

"Some of'em. We use'em to coon hunt. We'd never git out to them dogs if we didn't. I got a couple of'em that can jump a wire fence while you ridin'em.

"I've heard of jackasses that could do that but I've never seen it," Burke said. "So how do we do this?"

"Put a rope bridle on'em and bareback'em."

Burke looked at Frazier and gave a half sigh. "What the hell," he said, "We've tried about everything else. Why not jackasses?"

CHAPTER FORTY-SIX

For Lily and Isa, the uninhabited southeast corner of Choctaw County was almost more than they could bear. Although their survival instincts had grown exponentially, they were understandably restricted. Not one of their recent experiences up to the present had prepared them for the sky rocketing heat and humidity levels of being near the confluence of the Red and Kiamichi Rivers. Real nourishment was nearly non-existent. The biting horse flies were dive bombing them at will.

They had wondered beyond *Shangri-la,* finding themselves completely marooned from the seemingly endless fields of hay, fruit and vegetables. Even the bitter tasting horse apples would be acceptable.

There was plenty of water in the blowouts but the severe slopes made them too treacherous to reach. There was little else in the way of water, the naturally flowing creeks and ubiquitous ponds they had become accustomed to were replaced with the dry bed of Doaksville Creek. At least shade was plentiful, the canopy of Oaks and Maples providing a breather for them until something better came along. They intermittently leaned against the trees to rest for a few moments, then ate the pungent tasting leaves by twisting them off the low hanging branches. They even tried pulling the oak and cedar seedlings from the ground but found little if anything of value in their roots.

They had spent the previous night whimpering, at least at first, before all out trumpeting, as if willing to expose their location in exchange for food, water and the one thing they sorely missed the most, *air conditioning.* They had begun to sleep more restlessly with each passing night and napped even less during each day. In essence, they were dead or their feet. When they did finally find themselves horizontal, they could barely return to their feet. The simple task of moving was becoming more arduous. With their strength zapped, their huge bodies no longer barreled through the thick tree stands Still, they managed to make some progress. They had to. They had to eat more than just leaves. They had to find water or they couldn't last.

The water was out there, they could smell it, and their trunks never lied. But following their noses toward the river was problematic; they were forced to choose the path of least resistance which kept them plodding toward the east, away from the river, toward McCurtain County. In their condition, it was out of the question. They had to find their way south.

The Red River, flowing west to east about three miles away south of them, would be a short stroll for healthy elephants but an eternity for weary ones. It was the river that could be blamed for the dense and nearly impenetrable forest they found themselves in, having covered the bottom land with flood waters hundreds of times over the centuries. The last humans to venture into the area were the rock crushing crews, albeit equipped appropriately with thick clothing, insect repellent, trench hoes, front loaders and massive earth movers to do the job. It was seldom a bobcat or wild boar wandered in there and if they did, they chose not to linger.

For Lily and Isa, it was as if someone was dimming the lights, and the party was just about over.

CHAPTER FORTY-SEVEN

Wade Hammonds, Lyle Crockett and "Curly" Shirley Ray traveled county road E2080 east before turning south onto N4420, a dead end road wandering parallel to and within a half mile north of the river. It had been carved out by the rock crusher's trench hoe years ago and traveled only by hunters in their all terrain vehicles these days.

Crockett's 1970 green Ford Bronco bounced along rather easily with Curly falling considerably behind in the large square box van housing Juliet. Only a half mile in and Curly began honking and flashing her lights to get Crockett's attention.

He stopped in the middle of the road, looked down it and then to both sides before he and Wade walked the 100 yards to where Curly had pulled up.

"What's the problem?" Crockett asked through the truck's window. "We goin too fast?"

"Goin' too far," replied Curly, "I don't know how we could even git this thing turned around to get back out if we go much farther. I'm gonna have to back outta here."

"She's right," Wade said, looking at Crockett. "It's only going to hold one elephant at a time. I doubt we'd want to try and back this rig up several miles, especially more than once.

"Can we walk her down?" Crockett asked, referring to Juliet.

"We could do that."

"How far can she go?'

"Further than I can!" Curly snorted rubbing on the ample roll above the belt of her blue jeans.

"It'll take a little while longer but we should be all right," Wade replied.

"Let's throw the stakes and chains in the back of my truck," Crockett said. "I'll go on ahead until I find a roomy place where we can stake her in the shade."

"I'll come with you," Curly quickly volunteered.

"You'd better not," Crockett said. "If we were to find them, we'll need you in the truck. We may have to drive it down this road whether we want to or not."

"If we had to back it we could," Wade added. "I'd like to have three reasons to have to do it."

Curly and Wade opened the rear door of the truck and slid the accordion-like steel ramp to the ground, providing a long gradual slope for Juliet to walk down. Wade stepped up to the jittery elephant, patted her on the back left flank and uncased his bull hook. He only had to brandish it, never once touching Juliet with the point. She was trained to follow orders just from the mere sight of it.

Juliet backed carefully down the ramp and glanced toward Crockett as he started his truck. While Crockett backed the Bronco toward them to fetch the chains, she instinctively stuck her trunk into the air, familiarizing herself with the unusual surroundings. Had she smelled her friends, Wade knew she would more than likely trumpet for them. She didn't.

Wade made a clicking sound in his throat and put his hand on Juliet's side to indicate they needed to move. The two of them began a slow walk down the center of the road, Juliet swinging her trunk from side to side while Curly leaned against the truck's front bumper, one leg crossed in front of the other, lighting a cigarette.

Burke had convinced a grudging Whitley to act as their scout, riding the lead mule with the posse, now only eight left, counting Blue and Sponge. Actually, in Burke's mind it was only seven, since no one really thought Atwell would make it much further.

Each rider had a rope harness in their hand, walking their mules over the short clearing toward the thick several mile wide stretch of wooded forest where their search would begin and hopefully come to an end. Sponge walked behind, holding the reins for two mules, one for him and one packed with provisions and shelter.

Burke had prepared the men in advance; they were going to remain in the woods for as long it took to bring the elephant's home. He spelled out the rigors of the upcoming search in detail to Atwell. His only response was "Sheriff, I've come too far to turn back now." For the others, it was commonplace to spend several nights camped deep in the woods each deer season, they were prepared to treat the search for the elephants as such.

Near the entrance to the forest, the group was given a quick mule riding and handling lesson by Blue along with a warning that their mounts could be expected to get contrary at times. If it happened, he discouraged screaming or kicking them in the flanks because it would only make them more stubborn. "You wind up havin' to tug'em off their ass," he said.

Watching Atwell being tossed backward onto the ground, then drug around as he tried to stop his mule from running was wildly amusing to the seasoned riders and even Atwell himself couldn't help but be amused. For a writer, it would be additional color he would add to his story.

Even for the others, riding a mule was unlike riding their horse. A horse and rider usually had a trusted relationship and as they quickly found out, the mules were not necessarily in sync with them.

Before long, Blue gave the order to mount up and stay single file once they negotiated the opening into the woods. The group stayed in the same order as they had previously. Within moments, they were squeezing through scrub oaks and blackjacks, riding around fallen timber, leaning under branches and at times, dismounting to walk their mule through.

There was no way to avoid the rips and scrapes from the endless presence of the low hanging limbs, thick branches and vines. All had streaks of light red blood oozing from their necks and arms until they covered them completely, disregarding the fact they were over heated.

The first priority was to find an obvious trail the elephants had created. Once found, they expected the behemoths would have cleared enough of a swath for them to proceed more easily forward. The fact they had no idea where the elephants had entered the woods or in what direction they were heading presented the biggest problem.

Chuck's guess was the elephants would drift south toward the river for obvious reasons. Burke suggested east since they had seemed to be keeping to that direction. Blue split the middle, pointing out the chances for the most food and water sources should be a combination of south and east from where they were and they all agreed to follow him.

Atwell had already been thrown off a second and third time while stepping over fallen trees, once stopping for several minutes to collect his bearings after striking his head on a small stump. He assured the Sheriff he was alright and insisted they continue, only now he was following Sponge and the pack mule in the rear.

An hour in and Ben Bob acknowledged he wasn't feeling well, sweating profusely and becoming nauseous. After stopping several minutes to rest, he told Frazier he didn't think he could continue. He was feeling tightness in his chest and feared he may be having a heart attack.

Frazier looked at Burke as if to say he had to go. Cowboy volunteered to accompany Ben Bob out of the woods via the way they came. This was no time or place for taking chances and Burke asked the others if they wished to continue. Once he was assured they did, he radioed Mullin to have an ambulance for Ben Bob waiting at Blue's house. Cowboy reassured Ben he was going to be okay, wrapping wet bandanas on his head, neck and stuffing them inside his shirt before helping him back on his mule.

Sponge offered to help with the rescue but Ben waved him off.

"Good," Blue said. "He's the best cook here!"

"He's the only cook here!" Frazier said.

The six of them continued to look for clues, branching out in pairs to cover more ground whenever the clumps of trees and vegetation relented.

The slow going was quickly using the available daylight and with darkness approaching, Blue suggested they begin looking for a spot to set up camp. The limited light would make the prospect of falling into a blowout far too likely. The search would have to wait until dawn.

Burke stubbornly wanted to keep moving a while longer but was convinced otherwise. "Them two elephants are likely movin' slower than we are," Blue surmised, "and I'm worn out."

CHAPTER FORTY-EIGHT

Sponge sat on a stump with small sacks of potatoes, onions, jalapenos and tomatoes lying next to his left foot. He unfolded a large piece of tin foil and began tearing it into squares placing them onto the ground next to his sacks. He stiffly stood up, a byproduct of a long day on the back of a mule, and walked to the pack mule, pulling a clear cellophane bag filled with soft beef jerky from the side saddle. Once he was back on the stump, he flicked open his Gerber hunting knife, pulled out a large potato and began to slice it in silver dollar size slivers, leaving the skin on.

Burke, Chuck and Frazier, without prompting, gathered small branches and broken limbs to use as campfire kindling, certainly not because they needed the warmth as it was still muggy even in the fading daylight, but as a place for Sponge to cook his Shepherd Pies.

Atwell folded a blanket over the thick trunk of a fallen tree and benched himself, shifting uncomfortably from one buttock to the other to lessen the aches. He had become far less inquisitive, sitting bent over with this forearms resting on the tops of his knees.

"You okay Mr. Atwell?" Sponge said looking up from his peeling.

"Yea, just tired I guess."

"This heat'll shore take it out of ya," Sponge replied. "You probly not used'ta this."

"That shouldn't bother me, I jog 2 miles every day at lunch back in New York."

"What's jog?" Sponge said with a slight raise of his voice. "You mean that runnin' round city folks do?"

"Gotta stay in shape Sponge," Jack said as if he were doling out advice.

"I tell you what, you ain't gonna see me joggin', I wanna be sick when I fall down and die."

"Good one," Atwell said letting out a slight laugh.

Atwell had caught the attention of Hugo residents over the prior couple of days by zipping past them in his Nikes, snug running shorts and New York Yankees tank top. He was obviously in great shape and spent his time in Hugo not only working out and interviewing people but borrowing a dirt bike and riding with his co-reporter around some the areas where the elephants had been sighted. His female co-reporter Tannehill only lasted 90 minutes, choosing to rely on her rented Chrysler to finish her assignment.

"Philip, you don't seem like you're getting the hang of this," Burke said after overhearing the conversation between him and Sponge.

"Call me Phil and you can lose the smirk Sheriff," Atwell huffed, "I'll be alright."

Blue wadded up several handfuls of dry leaves, piling them beneath the kindling to start the fire. He applied a flame with his Zippo lighter, fanned it a little with his cap and quickly the smoke and fire from the leaves rose through the small tee pee shaped pile of limbs before bursting into flames.

"A Zippo?" Atwell said jokingly. "I thought you guys rubbed two sticks together out here?"

"You been watchin' too many Clint Eastwood movies," Blue snapped.

POW! POW! The sound of a .44 Magnum firing only a few feet from his right ear caused Atwell to slide off the log and lay half hidden alongside it. "What the hell?!" He was looking at Frazier opening the chamber of his pistol to reload then scanned the others who were all looking at Frazier, startled as well.

Frazier hadn't been seen since they began pitching camp, and he eventually looked up. "Copperhead," he said.

Atwell scrambled to his feet, backing several feet away, "Where!?"

"Don't worry, he's dead. He was curled up right at the base of that log you're sitting on," Frazier said while grabbing a stick to pick it up. "Good thing you didn't sit on the end of that log."

A dazed Atwell limped back over to sit down, first looking around both sides of the log for any of the snake's companions.

"Don't worry, they're loners," Frazier said.

"Where'd you learn to shoot like that?" Atwell asked.

"About four years old, right after I learned to rub two sticks together," Frazier remarked.

"Why you limpin'?" Sponge asked Atwell, gesturing at his leg with his paring knife.

"I hurt it a little on that second fall. It's okay."

"It don't look okay," Sponge said, "looks like its bleedin'."

Sponge placed his knife and onion on the towel in front of him, "Let's have a look at it," he said while getting up.

He pulled Atwell's left pant leg up to his knee, exposing a calf covered in blood from a three inch long gash. "Dang, there's 'nuff blood comin out of dat to paint a barn wid." Sponge said. Atwell's sock was soaked with blood.

Burke came over to take a look as did Chuck. Sponge went over to the pack mule, poured water out of a canteen over a clean red bandana, and then pulled out a leather pouch. He picked up his knife, using it to cut off his right shirt sleeve, before tying it in a knot below Atwell's knee. "We gotta clean it up," he said, wiping his calf with the wet bandana.

He pulled a jar of clear liquid out of the pouch and began unscrewing the lid. "What's that?" Atwell asked.

"Moonshine. Hold still."

He poured a large dose of the pure grain alcohol directly into the wound, causing Atwell to grab the top of his knee with both hands and jerk it back toward his chest. "Jesus God! That hurts like hell!"

"It's gonna make it feel better," Sponge said in a tone that indicated he had a bedside manner.

"When?" Atwell said grimacing. "Ow...Ow! Ow..." as he felt each wave of stinging pain from the alcohol. Sponge dried the area around the wound, then began pushing the sides of the gash together as closely as he could, applying two elastic bandage strips to hold it together.

"These oughta hole it for a while but you gonna need a doc to get it sewed up," Sponge said.

"We need to take him back to the house?" asked Chuck.

"No way. Not tonight. I doubt you'd find your way outta here in the dark without dogs," Blue said, referring to his coon dogs.

Sponge cut off the other sleeve of his shirt, exposing the second of his well developed biceps, soaked it with the Moonshine and lightly wrapped it like gauze over the top of the bandages. He helped Atwell to his feet then laid him down on the sleeping bag that Chuck had spread on the ground, propping his leg above his heart on the log. "That'll slow down the bleedin'. You stay right there an I'll finish fixin' supper."

Atwell put his forearm across his forehead and closed his eyes. "Looks like I owe you a shirt Sponge," he said. "Thanks."

"A waste of good 'shine if you ask me!" Blue huffed.

"You're lucky I don't throw you in jail!" Burke chimed in with a smile.

"Hell, if you threw everybody in jail that had a jar'a shine around here there'd be nobody left in the county."

"I'll leave that to the revenooers," Burke said, winking at Blue.

"Revenuers?' Jack said his eyes still closed.

"The U.S. Marshalls and DEA. Blue's their problem, I got other crooks to catch," Burke said.

Sponge finished mixing up the Shepherd's Pies, placing the six foil pouches around the smoldering wood coals on the edges of the fire.

An hour later and after a couple of pulls each from what was left in Sponge's *medicine jar,* it was time to eat the hot and delicious mish mash of vegetables, peppers and beef.

Frazier finished his portion then immediately laid back on his sleeping bag. He took off his .44, placing it next to him. "No false moves gentlemen," he joked.

"Who wants dessert?" Blue asked.

"Dessert?" Chuck asked. "Did Sponge bring a Dutch oven on that mule too?"

"Better'n that," Blue said.

Sponge walked back over to the mule, bringing back an even bigger leather pouch. He pulled two Mason Jars out, one with contents that appeared light brown and the other dark orange.

"Apple Pie or Dreamsickle boys!" Blue beamed, looking in Burke's direction and winking.

"I didn't see this," Burke said.

"My old Grandpa's recipes. Best damn white lightnin' you ever tasted." Blue said proudly.

He unscrewed the lid of the Apple Pie and took a large swig. "Damn that's good," he said wiping his mouth on the back of his sleeve.

They passed the smooth concoction of moonshine, blended with apple cider and spices, around until the six of them had finished the jar off. Even Frazier sat back up to take a few turns. Then it was on to the

Dreamsickle, another sweet flavored Moonshine blended with orange, vanilla and sugar.

No one was sure after that what went out first, the fire or them.

The posse had already started the process of building their camp about a mile and a half away when Crockett threw out the stakes and chains under a grove of large trees, then unrolled a couple of bales of hay out on the clear spot beneath them. Afterwards, he took off in his Bronco headed south.

Wade found the spot soon thereafter, pounded in the stakes and hooked up Juliet for the night. He still had no idea if the ploy would work. He had baited traps with *live bait* for just about everything you could think of: beaver, coyotes, hogs but never for elephants.

He walked back to the truck, sitting on the front hood next to Curly. "If they're close enough to pick up her smell, they'll come for her I think," Wade said. "Depends which direction the winds blowin'."

"No tellin'," Curly said flicking the ashes off her cigarette. "No tellin'."

"Well they ain't going to come anywhere near us if they smell those things," Wade said pointing quickly to the half smoked cigarette between her two fingers.

"You want one?" she asked.

"One, then we're done."

"The longer she goes staked out alone like this should have her crying out a little, they could hear her even if they don't pick up her scent." Wade said, while lighting up.

"I feel sorry for her," Curly said. "She's one of my babies."

"I'll take her some fruit and fresh water later and check on her. Can't let her feel too lonely," Wade assured her.

Wade climbed off the hood, leaving Curly as she lit another cigarette from the butt of the one she was finishing.

"Hey!" Wade said.

"You said one more," Curly said. "This is one more."

"That's it," he said wagging his finger at her as he opened the door on the passenger side of the truck. He stepped up and laid back for a short nap before it was time to go check on Juliet.

Curly finished the cigarette while she sat staring into the darkness and listening. After a few moments, she looked behind her at the sleeping Wade in the cab of the truck. She reached for the pack of Winston's lying next to her, lit the last cigarette she had left, crushed the package and tossed it onto the ground.

Crockett rolled slowly down the almost indistinguishable road, one that meandered in several directions, like a crack on a windshield. He had seen zero signs of the two during the hour or so of daylight he had available after depositing the stakes.

Once he reached a point that was easily a mile or more from Juliet, he stopped the Bronco, shut off the engine and sat quietly next to his rolled down window. Without the lights and nestled next to the tall rows of trees, it was pitch dark.

The night sounds, the most pronounced of which were Katydids, green four legged critters also known as bush crickets, were emitting an amplified chorus of screeching sounds. The steady cacophony was soothing to some and annoying to others. All his life, Crockett had fallen asleep on summer nights with the windows open, listening to the Katydids and he was fighting the urge to doze off to them at the present moment.

To stay awake, he watched the magnificent show the fireflies had begun putting on just after twilight, using their conspicuous bioluminescence to attract mates or prey. The thousands of tiny light bulbs flickering from their abdomens reminded him of the mirrored ball he had seen during the one and only night he allowed his wife to drag him to a disco during a weekend in Dallas. The Bee Gees didn't hold a candle to George Jones or Merle Haggard he remembered telling her.

Once the fireflies dimmed their bulbs and took a spot on a leaf, he clicked the dome light on, reaching for his tranquilizer gun in the back seat. He laid it on the front floor board. He pulled down the sunshade, flipped out the mirror and checked the look of his round beige colored cloth hat with the U.S. Forestry service patch sewn on. He was decked in his matching tan Serengeti Safari short sleeve shirt, rip proof khakis and dark brown all leather Wellington boots. As a wildlife management director, he preferred the bush look, more often referred to as safari gear. At this particular moment, his quest and his look were perfectly suited.

CHAPTER FORTY-NINE

Lily and Isa had yet to pull themselves off rock bottom. Nothing had improved, nor could it when they could barely make themselves move. Without food, water and sleep, delirium was setting in.

They had inadvertently split further apart than usual, a result of their collective stupor. The weakened Isa had stepped on the edge of the jagged outcroppings of rock around the rim of a medium sized blowout, falling and sliding toward the murky water before coming to a halt only a few feet away from splashing in. Only the light of a half moon illuminated her steps as she struggled back up the incline.

Lily found her way to a two acre sized blowout with a crescent shaped rim forming a natural dam at the end. The smell of the water was so enticing; she threw caution aside, walking down the moderately sloping embankment. Once there, she found the water suitable and wild onions growing near the edge. She tolerated the pungent taste of the onion roots then foraged along the edge for more. She sprayed herself with lukewarm water for as long as she could before returning to the top to pursue her friend.

Isa spent the next couple of hours as if she was suspended in space. She was too sore to walk since her fall, too groggy to trumpet for help and finally succumbed to sleep.

Once Lily was hydrated, she ate her fill of roots and leaves, all which helped her feel more energized than she had in a couple of days. She chose to take a nap while standing instead of searching for her friend.

It was 3:20 a.m. on Burke's watch when he was jarred awake by the very clear sound of an elephant trumpeting in the distance.

He pushed up on his right elbow and listened. There it was again, then again and again.

Frazier and Chuck were still passed out from their over indulgence of dessert several hours earlier. He crawled over and shook them one at a time as he placed his hand over their mouths. He glanced over at Blue and Sponge, sleeping on each side of Atwell. They were out cold.

"What do you think?" Burke asked Chuck.

"They're lonely. In trouble, maybe?" Chuck said.

"Blue was right, they're out there," Burke said. "I don't think they're moving.".

"It's not too long before dawn. They should stay put until then," Chuck said.

"We're this close guys," Frazier said, holding up his thumb and index finger close to each other. "Let's go gett'em now."

"We'd never catch'em in the dark," Chuck said. "They can see in the dark as well as they can see in the light."

"Douse the rest of coals and we'll have the mules ready to go just before day break," Chuck said. "We'll leave those three to sleep it off."

The three of them were too keyed up to lie back down after putting the saddle blankets and bits on the mules. "Funny ain't it," Burke said sitting down on a tree stump.

"What's funny?" asked Chuck.

"These damn jackasses were able to get us closer than everything else we tried. Dogs, helicopter, horses, whatever," Burke said, "It just seems funny."

Crockett looked at the clock on his dash reading 3:20 a.m., pulling himself off the seat by grabbing the steering wheel. He had clearly heard what the others had.

He laid back in the seat to listen, clutching his gun to his chest and within fifteen minutes of hearing nothing else, dozed off.

Curly's long night of smoking cigarettes on the hood of the truck and watching was finally rewarded by the sound of the trumpeting. She jumped quickly to the ground and climbed up on the vehicles passenger's side to shake Wade awake.

"I hear'em!" she whispered loudly.

"Juliet?" he asked thinking that's where they may be.

"Further off."

"Okay, let's hope this time we gott'em," Wade stated. "Let's sneak down near Juliet and wait."

"Wait right?" Curly asked. "You're not gonna do that on-gah-wah shit again are you?"

CHAPTER FIFTY

Curly radioed Mr. Rose for reinforcements. They would need any additional manpower he could round up as well a larger tractor and trailer, one capable of hauling two elephants. As expected, Rose was beside himself. He was asking questions non-stop, not allowing her to answer them entirely before lobbing another. She diplomatically asked him to keep his questions to a minimum and she would address the situation with him after the truck was on its way.

She remained in the truck, watching Wade as he sprayed himself and the vehicle with Acorn scent, a substance he used deer hunting. Finding a spot well out of sight, he planted behind a clump of brush, about 200 hundred feet from where Juliet was staked. With the one bale of hay he had remaining, he scattered some on the ground around him and stuffed some of the straw inside his shirt and belt.

It was nearly dawn as Burke, Chuck and Frazier walked their mules silently out of camp, toward the area from where the sound had originated.

Before setting out, Burke tapped Blue a couple of times on the shoulder, attempting to wake him, only to receive a wave of dismissal. Blue saw the mounted mules through one open eye, determined he wasn't ready to charge, and whispered they would catch up later.

"You have a wounded soldier to take care of," Burke reminded him quietly.

Blue sat up, rubbing his face a few times but didn't speak.

"Keep that radio on you and we'll let you know if we need you." Burke said.

"Okay," Blue said groggily.

"Oh, Blue, by the way..."

"What?" Blue snapped.

"Thanks."

Blue promised to get Atwell safely out to where he could be transported to a doctor.

The ride was every bit as treacherous and onerous as the previous days had been with one major difference; the adrenaline rush had their hearts pumping 120 beats a minute. The mules were responding to the good night's sleep, energetically navigating the timber, troughs and fallen trees.

"My tongue feels like I licked the felt off the top of a pool table," Frazier said quietly, referring to the cotton mouth leftover from the moonshine.

"I've already drank my canteen dry," Chuck said wearily.

"Lightweights," Burke said matter-of-factly.

"You don't feel like shit?" Chuck asked.

"I've felt like shit for the last three weeks," Burke said, "A headache from a hangover is an improvement."

Frazier pulled his tranquilizer gun out of its sheath to check if it was loaded, then asked, "You think they'll pick up our scent and run?"

"I think they would if they could," Chuck answered, "But I think they may have had enough."

"What makes you think that?" Burke asked.

"Their trumpeting. They vary the sounds according to their emotions, anger, loneliness, fear, excitement, even for sex."

"Me too," Frazier joked.

"I've heard just about everything from elephants," Chuck said. "Those trumpets last night sounded pretty weak. Like they were tired and afraid."

"Too much of'a good thing," Burke said, "Happens to us humans too."

Rose and three people from his circus staff arrived in the only remaining tractor and trailer left on the grounds. It had been mothballed a couple of years ago and replaced with a new one. Now, it was kept as back-up while the several others Rose owned were touring.

Burke had been attempting to reach Crockett for his location. After the third attempt he gave up. He radioed Rose to check if he had heard from him. He hadn't.

"Where the hell's Crockett?" Rose whispered loudly as walked up to where Wade was hiding.

"I hadn't seen him. Doesn't he have a radio?"

"He isn't answering," Rose said, turning to Curly. "Can we go find him?"

"Too late for that. Burke is closing in and we don't need to be stirring things up out there," Wade advised. "If they run, maybe they run straight to Juliet."

"What if he's hurt?" Rose said.

"He knows what he's doing,' Wade replied.

"He took off south in his truck," Curly said. "I 'spect he's down near the river."

"Maybe he needs to keep quiet," Wade added.

Burke had requested an ambulance be dispatched from Hugo Memorial Hospital and it was waiting at Blue's house for the three of them to emerge from the woods, Atwell told the medical technician he was feeling faint, as if his head was spinning. The tech sized up the wound on his leg, telling him he was suffering from both the loss of blood and heat exhaustion. He gave him a large cup of water while sitting him on the gurney.

"I'm not sure I was cut out for this," Atwell told Blue from the back of the ambulance.

"Not too many are," Blue said. "You come back to see us Mr. Atwell."

"If I do," Atwell said thinking about it, "I'll lay in a pizza oven for a while to get ready for it."

"Come in November and I'll take ya deer huntin," Blue said.

"Thanks for helping me out fellas."

Blue and Sponge shook Atwell's outstretched hand and Blue told him if he came back he would get out the "really good 'shine, the one he called *Mary Jane's Insane Grain.*

Crockett had inadvertently left his radio in his Bronco when heading out on foot just past daybreak. He managed to move fairly swiftly through an area of trees standing wider apart than the posse was presented with.

Keeping an eye on the compass he held in the palm of his hand, he veered a half mile, angling south and east before staying due south on a course for the river another half mile away. He partially climbed trees to get a view of the straightest paths to take and stopped along the edges of the blowouts looking for tracks. It was clear he was in his element and enjoying every minute of the hunt. He doubted anyone in the county had enough experience to track the way he knew how.

His coordinates placed him six miles southeast of Fort Towson. Being near the river, it was little cooler than where he had been the previous day. He continually swatted mosquitoes that were out enjoying the coolness the same as him. It was still early and the stupidity of leaving his radio behind crossed his mind several times. He thought about returning for it but did not want to lose the time. He knew he was close. He had heard them crying out loud.

Without a way to call in reinforcements, he devised a plan B. He would just have to put them both down for a *light nap* with his tranquilizer darts once he found them, then hustle back to his Bronco to make the call. To rest, he climbed several feet up a dead scrub oak tree, causing an unnerved owl to vacate the large branch he wanted to sit on. From there, he could see the entire circumference with his binoculars while mindlessly fiddling with a small tear beneath the knee of his khakis. "So it's rip resistant and not rip proof," he muttered under his breath.

At a ninety degree angle to his left, he spotted a sizable path that looked as if a bulldozer had thrashed through it. Even at large as it was, it was at first unnoticeable until the sun had risen enough to illuminate it. It was obvious it wasn't left behind by the floods or wind.

He climbed down and was forced to walk in several different directions as opposed to a straight line toward the path. By the direction of the small trees and snapped limbs, he determined the elephants were on a fairly straight line and as suspected, that line headed straight toward the river.

Crockett felt a twinge of panic set in as he thought of them reaching river and subsequently emerging on the other side of it. Worse yet, the additional currents in the river from the recent rains could easily sweep the two young elephants downstream and potentially drown them. What a horrible way to end the search. No one had actually allowed themselves to imagine the hunt could end tragically.

Before moving forward, he again considered returning to his car and radioing for help. Bringing a boat down river could possibly dissuade the elephants from entering the water. Alerting authorities on the Texas side to be on the lookout would be a good idea. He knew there was no time for that. He was staying with plan B! He had to catch up to them before they could get to the river. Otherwise, at best it would be a whole new ball game on the other side. He refused to dwell on the worst outcome.

The three mule powered posse was nowhere near as close to the elephants as Crockett. Burke continued trying to reach him but calls kept falling deafly upon the leather seats of his Bronco.

Ignoring Wade's warning to wait near Juliet, Rose and one of his hands were standing by Crockett's abandoned Bronco when he informed Burke that Crockett's radio was left in the seat. He felt the cold hood over the engine, looked around in the back seat for the tranquilizer gun and called Burke to report Crockett appeared to have been gone a considerable amount of time and could be considered a lone wolf at present. One could only assume he was on to something.

The posse pressed on, still looking for signs, and still not seeing any.

"It would almost be faster if we just tie these things up and walk," Burke said out of frustration, not looking behind him.

"If we knew what else we had to deal with then I'd be more apt to say you're right," Frazier said. "But these things can climb up and down these hollers a helleva lot faster than I can."

"Damn, what I wouldn't give to be chasing an armed robber right now," Burke said, and left it at that.

CHAPTER FIFTY-ONE

Crockett reached the top of the rim on the opposite side of the blowout where Lily had been foraging the evening before. The morning was warming rapidly to another miserably hot day and sweat was pouring off of him, staining a circle around the brim of his hat and soaking through his shirt.

He stopped midway along the rim to scan the area through his binoculars. The bottomless canyon like blowout was at least two football fields wide with brackish water. To go around meant he would lose more time in his attempt to head them off prior to the river. He spotted a large portion of the flattened vegetation, an obvious resting place for something with the girth of an elephant. He had his next trail to follow but before he was able to move toward the flattened path leading away from the large spot, he saw a glimpse of something moving.

He trained his binoculars down the length of trail, watching intently for several seconds. He first saw leaves and limbs violently shaking in the tree tops. He wetted his index finger and stuck it in the air but never removed the binoculars from his face. There was little wind to speak of.

At the base of the trees, Isa was wrapping her trunk around the small branches, stripping leaves. She didn't appear in any danger or in any kind of hurry. He noticed something else; she appeared to be alone.

He moved along the rim slowly navigating the 200 yards necessary to get around it. He kept Isa in sight, never removing his eyes from her. He was standing on top of the south rim of the blowout, now less than 100 yards away from her but concealed by the bushes. On his rear with feet out ahead, he dug his heels in the dirt and leaned backwards, scooting down the ravine. The rustling of his decent was too loud. He stopped, waited a few seconds and continued, this time walking tarantula-like with his abdomen facing the sky, his legs bent at the knee and his arms backwards from his shoulders. He was unnecessarily holding his breath at times.

He stopped about 20 additional yards into his scaling, checking for Isa once again with his binoculars. She was still there. He scanned around near her looking for Lily before looking behind him along the top of the rim. He saw nothing besides Isa.

He continued his descent until reaching an area where the surface flattened and after checking for Isa once again, stood up. Although he wanted to, he thought better of brushing the dirt and grass off his pants. He was thirsty and equally mad at himself for not only forgetting to bring his radio but his canteen as well.

He lightly tip toed from tree to tree, hiding behind each and peering out. From the flatter vantage point, he had managed to lose sight of Isa but he would have heard her run and possibly trumpet had she detected him. He picked up a small handful of leaves and dropped them. Thankfully they blew behind him. He was upwind.

He worked laterally along the path keeping about 100 feet from it. He kept thinking she must have picked up his scent, at least becoming a little bit suspicious. If not, then why could no longer see her? He kept moving and hoping she was adjusted to the scent of humans and harbored no fear of them.

He heard the crunching sound of limbs and could see Isa within 90 feet of where he stood. She had been rest-ing the previous few moments against a tree trunk, a short nap after the lonely night she spent on the edge of the blowout. She opened one eye and then the other as she sensed company.

The spot where she was standing offered very little in the way of an escape route. She had only one exit, back the way she had come in. She stood, her trunk lowered to the ground, curling the tip of it around of a piece of limestone three inches in diameter. Her eyes were looking straight at the area where she perceived the approaching danger.

Crockett stood frozen at attention, giving the appearance of a khaki colored male statue erected in the middle of woods. Against his shoulder, he held the stock of the tranquilizer gun with his finger on the trigger. He knew better than to quickly aim and fire. He had to think about the situation. If he tranquilized her on the spot, how would they ever get her out of there? He thought about it for another moment, both he and Isa locked in place.

He moved only his eyes, first to Isa's left then to her right and back straight ahead, placing his eye in the scope. He had chosen a spot on her neck and waited for her left ear to flap forward. *Maybe they run a bulldozer through the woods, chain her to it and lead her out?* He was still thinking about the consequences of dropping her at this point. It no longer mattered, her ear swept outward, going away from the spot he had in his sights, POP! SPLAT!

The tranquilizer dart hit its mark. Isa jerked and turned slightly to face her pursuer. In a blink, she forcefully unraveled her rolled up trunk, sending the rock with deadly accuracy at Crockett's head. Fortunately, it hit squarely into the tree trunk he ducked behind. She moaned twice; mournful tones as if to say "I'm hurt. Please don't hurt me again."

He quickly reloaded, placed the gun on his left forearm and used a small limb to help brace his aim. The sweat was dripping off his forehead, stinging his eyes. He waited to see if one shot would do the trick. He picked out a spot on her rear left leg if the second round were to become necessary. He kept his aim steady, breathed in and out slowly, while keeping his finger on the trigger. His heart was pounding.

Isa backed pedaled a few steps, not a natural move, indicating the chemicals were working their way quickly through her system. She stopped, attempting a wobbly turnabout to face the cleared out path from where she had came. She began to tread down it, every step measured, each becoming more difficult. Crockett took off, trying to keep in stride several feet behind her, watching and waiting, wondering if he'd soon see Lily come to her defense. He stopped to consider firing a second round into her leg. He wouldn't get the chance.

Isa abruptly ground to a halt. It was so sudden, he was still looking at her through the scope of his rifle. In an instant, she turned completely toward him and in one motion charged, covering the short distance between them quickly. He dropped the gun, immediately darting into the trees and scaling a scrub oak as impressively as any coconut tree climber in Hawaii.

Isa stopped at the tree, peering up at him as if she'd treed a raccoon, seemingly satisfied that she had backed him off. She stepped back into the clearing, coming perilously close to the rifle on a couple of occasions but missing it.

Again she turned to slowly saunter down the path. Her unsteady gait left Crockett enough time to slide down cautiously, pick up the rifle and go to one knee as he aimed the dart at her voluminous back side.

SPLAT! Isa felt another dart in her upper right buttock. Turning again, she executed the same move as before and charged Crockett, whose only defense was to again duck into the trees and begin climbing. This time with his rifle over his shoulder.

Isa crashed through the clump of trees that had protected him the previous time, coming upon him before he could fully climb to safety. Crockett turned with his back against the tree, attempting to slide away from Isa and around behind it. He was sure he was going to have to make a run for it.

Isa watched him move but didn't attempt to follow him. Her eyes were watering, her head was drooping and the look on her face as she peered at him was as if she was asking "why are you doing this?" Then she bent her front knees, lowering herself to the ground, the second dart finally putting her out. She laid to her side and slowly shut her eyes to sleep.

Crockett was breathing irregularly and terrified. He was not familiar with the affects of the tranquilizers on such a mighty and magnificent creature. He feared he may have killed her. He looked around for Lily before kneeling beside her to listen for her breathing. He could still see and hear her labored breaths and breathed a sigh of relief. He walked north down the path and wearily climbed to the top of the steep incline where he had first seen Isa. He raised his binoculars and continued to look for Lily. There was still no sign of her.

"One down and one to go," he said to himself. As he retraced his steps in the direction of his Bronco, the entire confrontation kept replaying over and over in his head. He couldn't wait to give Rose the exciting news and of course, sit for an exclusive interview with Atwell about his life and death encounter.

CHAPTER FIFTY-TWO

The small town of Fort Towson hadn't seen this much excitement since its bank was robbed at gunpoint by Charles "Pretty Boy" Floyd over 45 years ago. That event garnered little in the way of headlines compared to Isa's capture just a few miles away.

The local newspaper and radio station in Hugo were fielding inquiries from around the country; the sheriff's office was inundated with inquiries as well as demanding new information on Lily. A press conference was scheduled by White for the next morning at the Hugo Chamber of Commerce with another press briefing planned that afternoon in Fort Towson. He announced neither Burke nor Crockett would be in attendance, for obvious reasons, as they were still in the woods. He did promise an appearance by Buster Rose.

THE OKLAHOMA ELEPHANT HUNT IS HALF OVER! Legendary CBS newscaster Walter Cronkite removed his black horn rim glasses as he closed his evening news report, smiled at the camera and reported "Tonight, it's one down and one to go in the Great Oklahoma Safari...Baby Elephant Isa has been returned home safely while her fellow fugitive Baby Lily remains at large...authorities say they are very close to finding her...let's hope so...good night."

ELEPHANT ISA CAPTURED, LILY STILL LOOSE! Isa's capture came early enough in the day to make front page news in several July 31, 1975 morning editions of newspapers across the U.S.

The Associated Press wired a 200 word story with a file photo of a two year old elephant to the scores of affiliated AP newspapers around the country. The copy boy at the *Tulsa World* sprinted to the transmitter when he heard the bells go off signaling significant breaking news was coming through.

The local radio station dispatched its remote broadcast van to the site just southeast of Fort Towson in order to conduct interviews with anyone that knew anything about the ongoing search. Within the first hour of their broadcast, at least a hundred or more vehicles began pulling in around them, stretching for several hundred yards on each side of the road. The circus staff itself seized upon the opportunity, selling hot dogs, soft drinks and cotton candy near the stations mobile booth.

Burke continued to rely on Deputy Mullin to handle official inquiries, who was gladly enjoying being in the limelight. The *Hugo Daily News* was working on their second ever *extra edition,* to be delivered that afternoon on the streets of Hugo and surrounding towns. The first ever was the assassination of John F. Kennedy in 1963.

Unfortunately for Phillip Atwell, his leg injury and dehydration prevented his being there for the big moment. Considering his weekly magazine had already gone to press, it no longer made any difference.

Blue and Sponge visited Atwell at the hospital, bringing him a jar of Moonshine for his trip home to New York. His wound had required 31 stitches to close. The doctor informed him he was lucky to have arrived there when he did or the consequences could have been much graver.

He was released at 11 a.m. with the local press conference about to begin. He asked his editor for permission to stay but was denied. There were *real* sports stories to be covered and he had other assignments.

Blue and Sponge drove Atwell to his rented car. They sat three across in the cab of Blue's faded red 1959 Chevrolet Apache pickup, Atwell riding shotgun. His flight from Love Field in Dallas, three hours away, was scheduled for 6:10 p.m.

As they drove, his gaze fell upon the variety of retail fronts of the small buildings along Broadway and then Main, the people talking to each other on the sidewalks, the packed booths at Vets Diner and the Best Café. "This is a nice little town you have here," he said, somewhat wistfully. "Being here has changed my life in a way."

"What kinda way?" Sponge asked.

"Only writing about sports makes you focus only on the person or the event, the bigger the better," Atwell replied. "The real stories are the people and places that surround it."

Sponge shook his head up and down while scratching the side of his chin. He didn't reply, just kept looking straight ahead, the subject a bit too deep.

"Then you should come back," Blue said as he pulled next to Atwell's car, parked next to the newspaper office. "There's plenty'a stories round here. Some of'em are even true."

"I may have to work for a different magazine if I do that Blue."

He climbed out of the truck, grimacing from the pain and stiffness that would take days to subside. As he closed the door, Sponge scooted over to the open window. Atwell limped toward his car, then stopped in the street to look back at them. "Blue, I should sue you for false advertising."

"Why's that?" Blue asked.

"You call that place of yours Halfway to Hell? It's *total hell.*"

Walter White introduced Buster Rose to a packed conference room inside the Hugo Chamber of Commerce building. He walked briskly to the podium, smiling largely and holding the palms of his hands out to quell the smattering of applause.

"Thank you. One of my baby girls is home!" He blurted out to another round of applause.

"We've already answered a lot of questions this morning so we're going to keep this brief," he continued. "We still have one more little girl to bring home!" Rose was sounding more like a politician than a circus owner.

"Let me start out by saying thank you for all of the support from the city, county and state that we've been getting these past three weeks. As I said, we have more work to do and once we have Lily home, believe me, we'll show our appreciation officially by having a big celebration."

With that, he began to field questions. "Yes," he said, pointing to a young lady reporter for the *Dallas Times Herald* on the front row.

"Can you tell us why you think the elephants have remained on the run for so long Mr. Rose? "

"On the run? Miss, they were lost."

"But wouldn't they rather be lost in the woods than found in a cage?"

Rose seemed startled, clearly not expecting the question. "Can we talk about something else? I'm not sure if the verbiage really matters. They've been gone quite some time now and they need to be home. Next?"

The television reporter from KTEN-TV in nearby Ada, Oklahoma, extended his cassette recorder closer to the podium and asked, "Can you tell us a little bit more about how Isa was captured and where she is now?"

"Isa is fine. She slept through the night under a close watch by her trainer Wade Hammonds."

"In her cage?" the *Paris News* reporter interrupted.

"As some of you know, Lyle Crockett, the Regional Wildlife Manager for the State of Oklahoma, was able to tranquilize her," Rose went on, ignoring the interruption. "It was unfortunate but without anyone else around to help he did what he had to do for her own safety."

"She put up quite a fight," the reporter said. "Mr. Crockett is on record as saying he was surprised when she confronted him."

"Well...," Rose said thinking.

"Have you ever had one of your handlers killed by an elephant?" the same reporter from the *Dallas Times Herald* blurted out before Rose had time to finish his thought.

White stood up from the table beside the podium. "Folks! Can you please keep your questions confined to Isa's well being and the ongoing rescue efforts for Lily?"

Rose put his mouth up closer to the microphone. "With these kinds of questions, apparently there's an elephant in the room more so than in the woods."

"Everyone is well aware they've been out there for weeks. What people want to know is what made them want to run away in the first place?"

"Who are you with sir?" Rose asked the reporter making the remark.

"Oklahoma City Times," he replied.

"Do you know a lot about elephants? Circuses?" Rose asked him.

"Only what I've read. That some have been treated cruelly."

"I assure you, that's not the case at Rose and Hahn." Rose said, beginning to regain his composure.

"An elephant in captivity cannot survive in the wild," Rose began. "For that reason alone it is imperative that we find Lily as soon as possible. Half of all elephants die of hoof disease whether they are in captivity or the wild. They need constant care. No matter what you may think, elephants are a vital part of the circus family. They're trained to perform just as any animal is, just as any human athlete is."

The group of reporters and city officials stood quiet and expressionless as Rose continued. "I've never seen or know of anyone being intentionally cruel to our animals or to anyone else's for that matter. Elephants have worked side by side with mankind for thousands of years, helping build ancient civilizations. Nowadays, they use their enormous strength and agility to erect the big top in towns all across America."

As he was going on, some were becoming restless, wanting to ask additional questions. "Mr. Rose," one of the reporters interrupted.

"Wait, please," Rose said holding out a stop sign with his hand. "The work they do today may not be considered as important and necessary as it once was, but I assure you it is. How many of you went to a circus as a kid with your family? Laughed at the silly clowns. Ate the salty popcorn and cotton candy. Watched in wonder and awe as the elephants walked into the ring, bigger than life and larger than anything you'd ever seen?"

"We all have Mr. Rose," the Dallas reporter said. "I can appreciate your love for the circus, you make it sound very romantic."

Rose started to go on but was halted again. "Can you tell us about the bull hooks, what they are used for?" the Dallas reporter asked.

"Can we get back on the subject of finding Lily?" White said from his seat.

"For all they do, our elephants are provided with the cleanest of quarters, around the clock medical care, given ample amounts of time for recreation and socialization with each other, fresh food and pure water. They never want for anything."

"Other than to get away," the Dallas reporter snapped.

Rose remained calm after her snarky remark. He looked around the room, each person clearly waiting for his reaction. "It's entirely possible that elephants are way to forgiving for what we put them through. Perhaps the same can be said for horses, steers, dogs, all of the animals that are trained to perform. You'll have to make your own judgment. That's not the point here today. Thank you."

"One more question," the Dallas reporter said, raising her hand.

"Yes?" Rose said dreading what she was going to ask.

"Why do you think Isa threw the rock at Mr. Crockett?"

Rose thought for second, and then said, "Maybe they aren't so tame anymore."

CHAPTER FIFTY-THREE

Sitting beside Isa through the night while she slept off the drugs, Wade washed her with clean water from the five gallon pale he had carried to the site; doctored and bandaged her dozens of nicks and scrapes; left her for only brief spells to look around for Lily then finally fell asleep on the ground next to her.

When he woke up he radioed Rose with his idea to stake out Isa where she currently was, fully expecting that Lily would most certainly come back to find her running mate.

After agreeing with him, Rose deemed it unnecessary to keep Juliet locked up in the woods any longer and had Curly transport her back to the circus grounds.

Isa slept restlessly, abruptly coming to at dawn. At first groggy and drunk-like, she attempted to stagger to her feet. Spotting Wade nearby, she hurried even faster to her feet but exhibited little in the way of wanting to run.

Wade put his hand on her side, brushing her thick skin and talking in very low and gentle tones. What wounds he couldn't get to on her left side, he dressed after she had stood for a few minutes.

An exhausted Burke, Chuck and Frazier, still searching for signs of Lily, navigated to an area within a half mile of Isa and again pitched camp as evening fell. Crockett remained in his Bronco near the river. They had heard parts of his story on their walkie-talkie, but were too tired to sit through it all. He spared them the details for the time being. Still, the perilous capture was stunning and they were surprised by the fact that he somehow managed to find and capture her singlehand-edly.

The target area was now centered upon where Isa was staked and a thorough search of the radius around it was underway. The now rested posse of three showed up early, with Chuck and Frazier going east and west respectively and Burke north. Crockett would remain to the south. Wade rigged up an extra long chain to allow Isa to roam more freely.

After a couple of hours, Burke was back and asked Wade, "No way she would leave her friend behind, right?"

"Not unless she's injured and can't."

"That's possible. There has to be a reason she hasn't come looking for her buddy by now."

"She knows we're here Sheriff. She smelled us and heard us a long time ago."

"So nothing's changed, we're still the enemy?"

"None of us have any experience with a tame elephant that has been in the wild for weeks. I would think there's plenty of reasons for her to consider us hostile."

Crockett, with his radio now attached firmly to his belt, checked in with Burke. He had edged his Bronco as close to the river as he could, continued to wait, watch and listen.

Frazier and Chuck had returned with nothing to show for their efforts.

Chuck had heard the conversation between Wade and Burke. "We can't take it for granted that she'll come find her," he said.

"So, in a herd of elephants, is it survival of the fit-test?" Burke asked Wade, "You think she may already be blazing her own trail?"

"I think if she was going to return to Isa she would have done so by now," Chuck answered. "An elephant will help others in the herd to survive but her first instinct is her own survival."

"If that's the case, we may need more than just us," Burke said. "And apparently we may need more tranquilizer guns."

"That's for damn sure!" Crockett said through the radio as he listened in.

"Maybe we do, but we don't have any more time to waste," Chuck said.

"Let's try it around here one more time before we decide on another strategy," Burke said. "Let's go to the river, have Lyle meet us, then split up, two of us go east and two go west?"

"Beats any suggestion I have. Let's hope like hell she hasn't swam across it." Chuck said.

"Or worse," Burke said, everyone knowing what he meant.

Wade settled into a cove of trees about 200 feet from Isa as the others slowly rode out of sight. Burke instructed him to remain silent if he spotted Lily and just click the button on his radio as if he were going to contact them. He would see the red light on his and notify the others to circle back.

CHAPTER FIFTY-FOUR

Lily's separation from Isa was yet to be so overwhelming that she could ignore the heavenly scent of flowing water nearby. As much as she wanted to make a mad dash and splash in, the sound of the voices she had been hearing kept her secretly hiding and calculating each move. The fertile bottomland was gradually producing a greater abundance of food along with a habitat more like the one she had become accustomed to earlier in her journey. A nice respite since she had just lived through *hell*.

It had been less than 24 hours since Isa was captured, too soon for the real longing and loneliness to sink in. For all she knew, Isa could be partaking of the same vast amounts of delicious fare she had been finding and they would no doubt meet up at a later time for a nap.

It was the middle of the afternoon when Lily arrived near the south shore of the Red River, its water flowing steadily, more so under the surface than on top, and winding its way to the Mississippi River north of Baton Rouge. The sun was radiating its oppressive heat, so Lily stayed mostly in the shade and stopped to watch and listen as much as possible along the way.

Sensing she was alone, she stepped into the shallows only a few feet away from the bank. Wading out until the water reached her belly, she began splashing it by slinging her trunk side to side. She drank in large gulps, filled her trunk dozens of times to spray her back and finally returned to shore.

After a quick dry in the sun, she pulled roots from the soft sand and munched on the heart shaped leaves of several small Sycamore trees growing nearby. After a few false steps under the thick tree cover, she quickly learned to use her trunk to determine the density of the bogs she needed to step through. Actual quick sand wasn't common to the area but deep mushy pits covered in moss had been known to swallow coyotes and feral hogs that had gone too far into them.

Her emergence from the deep woods, where she had begun to feel confined, was beginning to restore her energy. The softness of the sand and mud beneath her sore hooves felt soothing, the openness of the surroundings, and the new sources of food, all helped her put her longing for Isa aside momentarily. Whenever Isa did come to mind she trumpeted several times to communicate her location to her.

ERRRR-RURRRHHH! ERRRR-URRRHHH! The strange sounds young Scotty Clifton was hearing went on and on. Each becoming louder than the one before.

URRRHNNNHH!

The next sound was unlike the other, like a loud shriek and squeal with a sort of ringing at the end. He heard it several more times as he stood waste deep along the red clay of the river bank.

At five foot six and only 130 pounds, it wasn't hard for Scotty to keep low and out of sight. He bobbed down in the water with only his forehead and eyes above it, getting an alligator-like view of his surroundings.

The 17 year old and his family lived on the Texas-side of the river and what was a typical day of noodling for catfish, was suddenly halted by the unusual sounds coming from the other side of a slight bend in the river.

Ordinarily he would have had a buddy or two along with him, since the *sport* of noodling, the art of cramming one's fist into the mouth of a large nesting catfish and jerking it to the surface, most times required help. Clifton was usually more concerned with sticking his hand into a log full of poisonous Cottonmouth snakes than he was losing a fist fight with a catfish.

However, he was alone and about ready to jump back into his john boat and paddle away, before curiosity had the better of him.

He grabbed some exposed tree roots, using them to pull himself up the sheer three foot high bank. Lying flat on his belly, as if he were staying out of the line of bullets whizzing over his head, he listened for several seconds but heard nothing.

Crawling on his knees for several yards through the sand, he partly rose up and looked at as much of the bank and tree line as he could see in front of him. He moved sideways on all fours, like a fiddler crab, closer to the tree line and away from the river bank. There was still nothing he could spot.

He thought what he had heard was an elephant. He was pretty certain, even though he had only heard them before in movies and on television. As a country boy that was home schooled by his mother, he had no knowledge of the two celebrity elephants on the loose, so it made very little sense for him to think there would be one anywhere near Texas.

He stood up, continuing to move along the tree line, looking right, then left, ahead and behind him. He dropped behind a large mound of sand, peering over the top and there it was! The rush of nervous excitement was immediate. He recalled seeing elephants up close at the circus and even at the Dallas Zoo but in the wild? On the Red River? No bars or rings in-between? It was just him and the amazing sight of this beautiful animal sharing the same 100 yard strand of sand.

Hatari! He couldn't get the thought of the John Wayne movie out of his mind. He had watched it over and over,

The Duke rounding up wild elephants and rhinos. He had wished one day he could do it too.

The Swahili word Hatari translated means danger, but Scotty felt no sense of it. He could think of nothing else but to approach the docile looking animal, hoping to be his friend. After all, how much more dangerous could this thing be than wrestling a pissed off sixty pound catfish!

He stayed low and peaked as often as he could at the sunning and swimming pachyderm. As she exited the water for the trees, he stepped quickly out to the side of the mound to watch where she was going. He remained still, the last thing he wanted to do was scare her off.

Once she was out of sight, he walked closer to where she entered the woods, his bare right foot landing square on top of a sharp rock. He tried to muffle his reaction but the resulting OUCH! had Lily running from the trees and east down the shore.

He limped forward, screaming "NO, come back, I won't hurt ya fella!" But it was too late and he doubted the elephant spoke anything but Swahili anyway.

He ran back to his boat, leaving to tell his mom who would soon notify the authorities.

CHAPTER FIFTY-FIVE

The word that Lily was bathing in the river less than a mile away from Burke's posse was communicated to them in a round-about fashion. Scotty called the number for the Lamar County, Texas Sheriff's Department from the number his mother had stuck to the refrigerator. The Texas authorities notified Deputy Mullin, waiting on hold while Mullin finished yet another interview with an out of town newspaper. After three minutes, the dispatcher hung up and called back telling the girl answering the phone that the call was urgent.

Mullin wasted little time notifying Burke, who stopped his mule so the others could pull alongside to listen.

He listened intently as Mullin gave him the coordinates, and then asked Mullin to have the Lamar Sheriff dispatch several of his units to patrol as closely as they could along the matching area to the south side of the river.

Hearing the elephant had headed east along the bank, they decided to drop as straight south as they could, hoping to head her off.

Having no ride himself, Crockett was forced to ride double on Burke's mule. They each kicked their mules twice in the flanks and the scramble to reach the river's edge was on.

They hadn't gone much more than a quarter of a mile when Burke's mule had had enough, gravitating to his rear and dumping the two of them off backward. Burke tried to pull the stubborn mule to his feet but couldn't budge him.

Thinking quickly, Burke told Chuck to give his mule to Crockett so he and Frazier could go on ahead. They were the shooters. He and Chuck would get there as fast as they could.

A few minutes after they left, Burke's mule finally relented, standing erect. Chuck had gone ahead by foot and Burke caught him as he neared the river. They were only a couple hundred yards behind the other two.

They were nearing the area that Mullin had designated. Burke whispered to Frazier to proceed cautiously west and Crockett east.

"Find a place and hunker down," Burke told them. "Chuck and I will stay put right here."

The two marksmen rode toward their positions.

"I hope they won't have to shoot her with those things." Chuck said.

"Only if it's necessary." Burke replied.

"If we get close enough for me to talk to her she'll come to me."

Burke looked at Chuck a little curiously, looked down at the bull hook in Chuck's hand and said, "Really?"

For 10 minutes, Chuck managed to slither through the trees on foot, stopping on occasion to peel the thorny Greenbrier vines away from his jeans. He had almost tripped several times when he had become snared by them. He reached to his side, taking his bull hook from its sheath, and used it to knock away limbs and slash through the higher bushes

Frazier was encountering the same issues, his mule tangling up in the vines. He dismounted and kneeled down behind a tree near the river's edge.

Chuck kept walking and thinking to himself, over and over, "Lily knows me, she won't run."

She did.

Chuck stopped abruptly upon seeing Lily staring at him from 100 feet away. He tried to remain calm and called to her as quietly as he could, "Lily, time to go home girl." Then he slowly moved toward her. He made it to within about 15 feet when Lily noticed the reflection off the bull hook he had been trying to keep out of sight in his left hand.

She immediately began to back away, causing Chuck to quicken his step before tripping forward when his pant leg became wrapped in the Greenbrier. Lily continued in reverse until she was able to maneuver around and begin a westward dash along the river bank.

Chuck recovered from his fall and continued trying to communicate with Lily using familiar tones and clicking noises with his tongue and throat, sounds that indicated it was time to eat or to load up.

He couldn't tell if she actually could hear him. He had never had this kind of reaction from Lily before. It was apparent, after nearly a month, she no longer required a caregiver.

Not quite at full stride, she left the sand and headed to her right toward an opening in the trees.

PHHITTT! SPLAT! Crockett's dart had burrowed into her right flank. He had been posted about 150 feet behind Lily, along the tree line, and then moved in closer anticipating she would bolt in the opposite direction away from Chuck.

Lily veered away from the trees and back toward the water, picking up speed the moment she felt the dart's impact. She ran for fifteen more seconds, her rapid pulse helping to speed the chemicals into her brain. Her gait slowed to a slight jog and her legs started to become wobbly, the strength noticeably draining from her body. In another instant she was down, the subsequent thud cascading a thick plume of sand over her.

Crockett took off running down the bank yelling "Yahoo!" several times and nearly skipping. He stopped momentarily to load another dart just in case the same thing happened that happened with Isa. Chuck ran up to him, placing his hand on the rifle's barrel, pushing it away.

They watched her for a moment and were soon joined by Burke and Frazier, the four of them walking side by side toward her.

They were shaking each other's hands and patting Crockett on the shoulder. After almost four crazy, wild and agonizing weeks, it was *over!*

As they stood at Lily's side, they each said nothing. They could only look down at the fallen animal with admiration and respect. The exhilaration they were feeling at the moment would soon be overtaken by the exhaustion. It was so quiet, the river's flow could be heard as it flowed by. A large cluster of crows, perhaps sensing a kill, began returning to the trees after being scared away by the commotion.

Still looking down, Chuck put his bull hook back in its sheath, took off his cap and finally broke the silence, saying, "Don't tell Mr. Rose I said this, but I really can't blame her for wanting to be free."

Burke looked at him, raised his radio, took one more look at the sleeping giant and called Rose, "Buster, come get your baby girl."

Crockett pulled a Kodak Instamatic Camera from the pocket of his shirt, handing it to Burke, eager to capture the final moment of his big game hunt.

He positioned himself on one knee alongside the peacefully slumbering Lily, pulled the brim of his hat over his forehead, held his rifle to his side with the butt in the sand, smiled broadly and said "Cheese!"

Over the next couple of days, the photo of Crockett and Lily appeared in newspapers and on television newscasts coast to coast along with the headline, THE GREAT OKLAHOMA SAFARI IS OVER!

EPILOGUE

The following morning, White scheduled an afternoon press conference at the circus's headquarters, noting that Lily and Isa would be on hand, along with Sheriff Burke Blakemore, the Great White Hunter Lyle Crockett, and circus owner Buster Rose.

He promised a complete recap, their disappearing in one fell swoop, the weeks of searching, the people that helped bring them home and most importantly the current state of physical and mental health the animals were in.

Under no circumstances would they be taking questions from anyone, having learned their lesson from a couple of days ago.

The crowd at the conference was mostly city officials and well wishers. With the word going around that no questions would be addressed, it drew only a fraction of the media types which had practically camped out in Hugo for weeks.

Burke began by thanking the scores of people that had assisted in some way with tracking and ultimately capturing the two elephants before any harm could come to them.

He admitted that he, like everyone else, had found great amusement in the elephant's elusiveness at first but it quickly gave way to concern.

He directed a comment to White, telling him he had made his job easier, since the entire country was now aware of "little ole Hugo." He thanked the media for the admirable job they did in keeping the public informed.

"I mostly appreciate those in the media that actually came to Little Dixie to see for themselves the enormous amount of obstacles that had to be overcome in the pursuit of these elephants," Burke said. "For some in the media, finding out about the dangers and hardships these two tame elephants were encountering in Oklahoma wasn't near as funny as coming up with all the jokes and snide remarks."

Rose stepped to the microphone and kept his comments brief. "I would like to express my sincere gratitude to all of the people the Sheriff mentioned. Everyone should be aware, the health and welfare of these delicate animals were always our foremost concern and that part of the story is anything but amusing."

"Can you tell us anything we may not already have heard, regarding how they were captured Sheriff?" one of the newspaper reporters in the crowd asked.

"Isa's exciting capture has been pretty well documented in detail by Mr. Crockett." Burke said, "And since he was the only one there when she was, we'll have to take his word for it."

Crockett smiled and tipped his hat to the crowd.

"As for Lily, her capture was far less dramatic thank Goodness," Burke added.

Burke couldn't resist at least one more jab at the media, concluding his remarks by pointing out that the successful conclusion to the saga brought very few of the press back to town. "I guess a couple of sleeping elephants back home in their trailers wasn't enough blood and guts for the big city papers."

Rose again took the microphone and thanked most notably Burke, Frazier, Wade, Curly, Chuck and Crockett for their diligence and determination. He included his appreciation for his circus family of employees, the people of Hugo and Choctaw County as well as the State of Oklahoma for their help and assistance. He pointed out Blue and Sponge, referring to their cooperation and backwoods abilities to hunt and track. He mentioned he would buy Scotty Clifton a new fishing pole but he didn't think he would use it. Finally, he thanked the local newspaper and radio station for keeping people abreast of the ongoing situation.

What's next for Lily and Isa?" another reporter asked Rose, who was willing to tolerate innocent questions.

"On to South Texas and Mexico after a couple of days of R and R. That's where our show is now."

In the background just behind the stage, Lily and Isa munched on hay, carrots, cantaloupes and drew water from the multiple wash tubs to spray over their scorched heads. They seemed far removed from all of the fanfare that was going on in front of them.

Rose stood aside to present the two of them and stressed they had survived with only a few minor cuts and bruises from their trials and tribulations. "As you can see, they're good as new and extremely happy to be home!"

Perhaps it seemed that way to most everyone in the audience but that's not exactly how Lily and Isa *remembered* it.

ABOUT THE AUTHOR

JOHN S. WHITE has spent most of his career in the television and print advertising business, helping clients sell hundreds of millions of dollars in products and services. His true passion is writing, having hundreds of business and travel articles to his credit. Married and the father of three millennial daughters, John has lived in Oklahoma all of his life where he works and writes full time.

Made in the USA
Middletown, DE
27 July 2017